Bundt Cake

by Mireille Sillander

1.

"Put it out! Put it out now! What are you incompetents doing?!"

Cake was frozen in his tracks. He was still holding his glass of water in one hand and the thick stack of contract printouts under the other. The flaming Roomba sputtered around bumping into furniture. Panicking people were pulling their legs up, standing on chairs and screaming as the Roomba suddenly got its second wind and charged towards Mr Von Praeger. It wedged itself under his chair's legs, and with a furious whine started melting them. The room was rapidly filling up with smoke from the burning plastic as the previously screaming people were now stampeding out of the conference room, pushing and trampling anything in their path.

Then Mr Von Praeger's jacket caught on fire.

The synthetics went off like a lump of petrochemicals in a brilliant blue and green pyre. The fire quickly oozed on to the conference table, curling the meeting papers and making the ball point pens bubble into toxic puddles. Mr Von Praeger stood next to his jacket raging at the fire.

"Stop it! Stop doing that!" He flailed his arms in the general direction of the people escaping; "Come back. Come back, you cowards! You're all fucking fired! Do something!"

The smoke was now obscuring the conference room ceiling in a noxious black sea, and the raging had turned into a continuous scream as the jacket blazed with a fury of a thousand dead dinosaurs.

"AAAAAAAAHHHHHHAHAHAHAAAHHHHHHHR RRRRGGRGRGRGRGRR!!!!!!!!!!" Mr Von Praeger was pulling his hair, yelling at the fire to stop burning things.

Cake had finally decided to move and set his drink and contracts on a side table. The fire extinguisher was on the other side of the office in the break room. People responsible for installing it probably thought it was far more likely someone would set the microwave or the fridge on fire, rather than a volatile electric gadget, just by accidentally spilling water on it. They had been wrong.

He snagged the extinguisher and hurried back pulling the pin out while running. Pressing the trigger as he stumbled into the smokey room, Cake unleashed a gush of foam that spewed forth in a calming ocean, covering flaming papers and furniture in a white lather. Halfway through extinguishing the chair, the foam petered out into a trickle. Adrenaline pumping in his veins, he felt almost heroic as he pulled off his jacket and threw it on the heap, stamping out the remaining flickers.

The flames choked out quietly under his feet.

Cake stomped on the jacket a few more times just to be sure before stopping. He looked up with a wide grin.

There was an eerie silence in the office. Nothing moved but the gently drifting smoke pushing out from the jacket sleeves.

Cake straightened his back only to be met with a red and black Mr Von Praeger. His tinted sunglasses were now matte black as was his previously leathery tan. The veins on his neck were pulsating irregularly, and his entire upper body had turned to that critical shade of red everyone in the office knew meant someone was about to get fired until the third generation, though it was rare people set things in the office on fire.

"Uh... you have a thing..." Cake pointed at a dollop of extinguisher foam on the tip of his nose.

Mr Von Praeger's lips were pressed together so hard you could see his lower jaw turning white in a stark contrast to the soot on his face and the bright red inching its way up his neck.

"Do I now," he whispered almost without moving his lips.

"Yeah. Right... there." Cake booped him on the nose.

It wasn't the fire or the smoke but the variety of unheard of expletives that people remembered from that day. At least one book was later published simply detailing the words. It became an Amazon best seller for an afternoon.

Five minutes later Cake was sitting on the street curb looking at pigeons courting each other.

More pigeons kept dropping in.

This was the place to be for pigeons.

He dug out his phone and tapped the screen.

-I just got fired again-

The words hung there unsent in the void between reality and just now. If he didn't send them...

The message was hurled into existence with a flick of a thumb. He sat staring at the phone for a moment waiting for the **READ** to turn into **TYPING***,* but the message just floated there, check marks bright blue, unaligned like Switzerland. No one in the group chat would touch it.

People with hard shoes pounded past Cake as he sat holding his phone, ogling angrily at the blue check marks and the pigeons courting at his feet.

He stared at his phone.

The birds ruffled their chest and cooed at Cake's shoes. His mouth pulled into a thin line as the seconds stretched and the group chat remained silent.

Finally he turned the phone off and put it back in his pocket.

He squeezed the little plastic bag between his feet as the birds circled it, eyeing up it like formidable competitor. It was a bag of brand merchandise, mostly as a courtesy for having been there and done that and worked for exposure: a coffee mug, a mouse pad and a complimentary t-shirt. The company's logo was boldly emblazoned in gold on the side of the bag.

Cake rubbed his face and ran his fingers down to pull at the short stub of a beard he'd just started growing to fit in at the company. It had been an investment. An investment in time to his future as one of the people who belonged to that life, doing that job in that company. *Feels longer.* His beard had barely grown during the internship, but Cake was determined to hold on to the illusion it had. *Must be a half an inch since last week.* He rolled a few errand hairs between his fingers thoughtfully.

The pigeons were cooing mercilessly at his sneakers. Cake's hands dropped in resignation and he simply contemplated the birds for a good while.

The sun was starting to cast afternoon shadows over the sidewalk when he eventually grabbed the plastic bag and headed for the bus stop.

2.

The bus stop in the corner of Madison and Boulder Street looked like an industrial accident. This was on purpose. Even as the surrounding neighborhood progressively housed more and more wealth, the bus stop remained an eyesore for the sake of misjudged authenticity. No one ever stood under the bus stop. Kids would tell stories of all the diseases you could catch from simply walking past it. Cake didn't feel like wondering about the unaesthetic decisions today. He stomped past the stop and up the stairs of the overpass, with his little bag firmly tucked under one arm.

It was past 3pm and there was an endless stream of men in beer t-shirts and ironic mullets coming and going up the stairs with their electric unicycles. They were followed by women sporting near invisible bangs. The Boulder Park area had been heavily gentrified in the past 5 years. It had originally been a working class suburb that started to get more and more useless, empty office spaces when the working class people living there had gotten better wages, and moved out to houses with lawns and fences. The tall, gray, angular apartment buildings had always been uglier than sin, even when they were first built, to

8

match the bus stop. The bakeries and delis of the area were something else though. It was a truth universally acknowledged that it was a good idea to sell take away food in places where shift-workers lived. The bakeries baked and the delis prospered as fresh burgers, sandwiches and rolls were devoured by hungry workers around the clock.

Cake had briefly lived here with his mother and older brother right after his parents divorced, but after the paperwork went through and mom had gotten another job, they quickly moved on. It wasn't much of a place to raise kids even if it there was always fresh bread. Still, some of his best memories came from Boulder Park. He'd been a cute kid and no shop keeper could resist a lonely cute child with a big appetite.

He crossed the street again and headed towards a red brick building a few blocks away. A pasty man with a head like a toe, wearing a red cap and a white polo, rushed past him with a box of Talina's cupcakes almost crushed in his hands. The man barely missed Cake and gave him a filthy look. *Fuck you too, buddy.* Cake pulled a sour face back and wished the man would stub all of his toes on a side-table.

Talina's bakery was still the most popular place in the neighborhood. It had been for over 20 years. Talina's bakery wasn't called that though; it was Mrs Susan's Sweet Shop. Susan was the previous owner. Talina had come in when she was still known as Raman and worked there right up until Ms (she'd never been a Mrs) Susan had retired. She'd decided to invest her savings and bought the place. After some minor modifications, it was now also a coffee shop that sold the best milkshakes... well, anywhere Cake knew. Granted, Cake hadn't been everywhere, but if there were better milkshakes sold somewhere, he was sure he'd have heard about them by now.

Cake stormed through the door making sure everyone knew he was a man with baggage, with his shoulders hunched and face drawn, looking at least 5 years older than his 25. He scowled around the cafe, letting his eyes adjust to the dim interior light as a hush settled over the crowd. *That's right, don't mess with me,* he squinted at them. The hush quickly disappeared as nothing interesting happened, and people went back to their pastries and lattes. Cake slumped on a bar stool and slammed his palms to the counter.

"Talina! Hit me!"

Talina was a big, round woman with soft brown skin and stick straight hair tied in a braid at the nape of her neck, then folded over three times. On most days she wore bright red or purple under her apron. Her nose was regal and her fingers wide, weighed by carefully selected gold jewelry. Each piece was significant, she'd told Cake. In reality, only two were significant and the rest she was just very pleased to have picked up when they were on sale. She was putting away her broom in the closet when Cake barged in. Today she was wearing purple.

She eyed Cake silently for a moment. "Bad day." He nodded. "How bad?" she raised a perfectly plucked eyebrow at him.

"Double Trouble," Cake growled, coughed at the strain, then leaned his face in his hands and let a long sigh deflate his body. His hair flumped gloriously over his fingers.

The sounds of the coffee shop started to penetrate his hard imposed bubble of misery. Little pieces of other peoples' lives he had been pushing out of his mind. The group of bemulleted men at the back of the shop hyucking to themselves, skateboard wheels lazily whirring against the floor, porcelain cups hitting tables and spoons clinking in coffee. A baby bursting out crying. The baby's mother was having a coffee and a heaping slice of pie with another woman with two identically soft, bald creatures. It took two minutes for all three to be crying in unison. Both women continued eating their pie with chilling efficiency and used their free hands to rock their strollers.

Cake glanced over his shoulder at the wailing, and closed his eyes. When he turned back, an old lady sitting two seats from him gave him a sympathetic eye roll.

"You don't have one of those, do you?!" she said, pointing at the babies with a fork.

"No, ma'am," Cake said.

"Good! Keep it that way! Don't fall into the trap! Once you have kids, you'll never get rid of their father! You'll be stuck with the fucker until one of you dies!" She paused. A light seemed to go up in her wet little eyes and she set her fork down, pulled out a piece of paper, and quickly scribbled something on it. Then she folded it neatly and put it in her skirt pocket. Returning to her plate of petits fours, she stuffed a large one with a strawberry cutout on top of it into her mouth.

Cake shook his head and turned back to stare at the counter. It was a rustic wooden thing. It had dimples and grooves and old knife marks like a proper wood counter should. He ran his hand over the surface, fingertips feeling out the grain under the lacquer, briefly wondering where Talina had gotten it. Mrs Susan's counter had been solid beige Formica.

Talina interrupted his misery with the first half of Double Trouble; A tall, 24oz chocolate mocha milkshake with a Nutella-crêpe stuffed in the middle, topped with two different flavors of whipped cream and pink chocolate sauce. The rim had sprinkles and a fresh chocolate chip cookie wedged on it like a slice of lime in a cocktail, if the lime was baked and deep fried and also delicious. She'd stuck a straw through the sea of whipped cream.

"Sorry, we're out the blue ones with the sparkles," Talina smiled wryly. "I'll have to go get the cake from the back. Had a lot of traffic today," she sighed and disappeared through the kitchen doors.

Cake took a long, lingering sip through the straw. The chocolate milkshake rushed on to his tongue and spread like a sweet, soggy carpet right down his throat, triggering a cascade of delightful serotonin eruptions as the milk, the ice and the freezing cocoa clashed together against his worn nerves. "Delicious" he whispered to himself. The nubby tentacles of shame flickered at the edges of his consciousness – money, career, healthy coping mechanisms — but Cake brushed them aside. "I deserve this," he mumbled. *I don't care*.

He pulled the cookie off and crammed it in his mouth whole. The warm, gooey chocolate danced on his taste buds, telling him comforting things. But it wasn't enough. He needed something more.

Talina returned from the kitchen with the second half of Double Trouble on a plate: a four layered chocolate fudge pecan praline cake with a thick layer of pistachio icing and thin mints on top for decoration. The cake itself was always impressive but she'd gone an extra mile and added dark chocolate sauce and a dollop of vanilla custard in a little cup on the plate.

Cake's eyes lit up. Simply the sight of it made the day seem a little brighter.

"I put in a little---," Talina started but Cake had already sunk his fork in it and stuffed a good fifth in his mouth.

"--- vanilla custard there for you."

Cake glanced at the cup and nodded, his cheeks bulging with chocolate and thin mints.

"Mh-hm," he continued nodding while concentrating on shoveling more cake into his mouth.

Talina lifted a finger, then stopped. She leaned back and crossed her arms across her chest.

"Ok, so what's this all about, Cake-boy?"

Cake looked up from his cake with a wild expression of an over-caffeinated deer in headlights. There was so much sugar. He could feel the ticking of a tinnitus starting at the back of his head and knew there would be consequences. But he didn't care. He swallowed.

"I got fired."

"What?!," Talina shot up. "How can they fire an intern?! Were you even getting paid?!"

Cake shrugged and went back to shoving cake into his mouth.

"Ok, what did you do?" Her voice was firm and skeptical. She crossed her arms again and shifted her weight to one leg.

"Put out a fire," Cake said moving crumbs along the plate with his fork.

"Aaaaaand...?"

"...maybe start a fire...," he said almost inaudibly.

Talina sighed.

"Anyone could've started it!" Cake pouted. "The Roomba was obviously defective if it couldn't take a glass of water on it," he gestured with the fork his voice going up an octave. "And it's not like I poured the water on it on purpose." He picked another thin mint off the cake with the fork and placed it almost delicately in his mouth. The cocoa was doing its job cheering him up in just the right way. But none of that was, of course, going to bring the internship back. Which meant many things he didn't want to think about. "And it definitely wasn't my fault it burned Mr Von Praeger's jacket. Or that it was his favorite jacket. I think all jackets are his favorite jackets."

"Oh child...," Talina let out. "Here I was worried someone might've died."

"Well, I'm out of another internship and out of a job, a possible side-job connected to this one, and I don't know exactly how I'm going to pay next month's rent, or food, and Mr Von Praeger is going to make sure it'll be really REALLY hard for me to ever work within 100 mile radius of any West Coast marketing department," Cake continued.

"You don't think you're giving him a bit too much credit now?" Talina leaned on the counter with her soft, round hands.

"No," Cake said. "Ok, maybe. Just let me have this?" He looked up pleading. "I gotta have somewhere to direct my anger and frustration when I get pretty fucking big obstacles with ten thousand dollar debt tags sprung on me like this." He took a big bite out of the Nutella crepe. The crepe spilled its contents on where his beard should've been. Since the beard had failed to materialize, his chin took most of the damage.

Cake sighed. This day wasn't about to give him a break.

"Look, if I don't have at least a six month internship, I wont graduate. Again. It's not just that the vindictive fucking hobgoblin is going to blacklist me in all fashion magazines from here to, I dunno, Canada? I'd also need money... you know, for foods and stuff. Basic living," Cake waved the crepe around in his hand. "And pushing back the degree yet another year... fuck." He leaned on his elbows and looked thoughtfully at the limp crepe. His chest hurt.

"You need a job?!" the old lady from the next seat piped up.

"Uh... yes, ma'am." Cake turned to her.

"Come mow my lawn!"

"Thank you. That's a very kind offer, ma'am, but I don't think I can be mowing your lawn every day now." Cake attempted a sympathetic smile. A glob of Nutella dropped to his lap from his chin.

"I'll pay you twenty bucks!" the old lady cheered. Her eyes were so small and hidden under layers and layers of wrinkly skin that it made her face look like a badly folded origami. Cake was now genuinely curious what she might's have looked like before the wrinkles had set in. The abundance of skin didn't leave any clues of it. Her cheekbones were high and sharper than a paper cut and her wispy white hair was tied in a braid that circled her head. She had on a skin-tight dress shirt in a hypnotic 1960s pattern in browns and yellows, and a caramel colored skirt. She was tiny enough her feet didn't reach the foot rest, so she merrily swung them back and forth in the air like an excited 5 year old while eating her petits fours.

"This is Miss Gertrude Bannister," Talina nodded to her with a smile. "She's been coming here since Susan first opened the place."

"Really?" Cake's brow furrowed. He was trying and failing to remember if he'd ever seen the old lady there when he was a kid. "Twenty bucks?" he repeated. "Ok, you got yourself a deal, ma'am."

"Good! Problem solved! Come over tomorrow!"

Cake grinned solemnly.

"You need more than twenty bucks?" Talina asked quietly with a sympathetic head tilt.

"Yeah...," Cake sighed slumping back to his seat.

"I'm not making any promises, but I'll ask around." Talina whipped out her cell phone.

"I'd really appreciate that. The 2 bucks an hour the fashion goblin was paying me for covering their mail room after interning hours, was barely covering rent. Savings are almost done for." Cake rubbed his eyes and felt something wet on his eyelid. He looked at his palm and saw a long smear of Nutella across it.

"Phone sex?" Talina asked flipping through her phone.

"Excuse me?"

"It might not be the biggest paycheck, but I got the phone number right here." She held her phone up.

Cake squinted at the screen.

3.

The street lights had already lit up Rose Hill as Cake moseyed up his home street. The sidewalk was still radiating heat from the day as he got off the bus, but the evenings were already getting chillier. There wasn't much of summer left before the leaves would start to turn and people would layer on more and more clothes in an effort to deter winter. Winter wouldn't care. It would still rush in unexpectedly with runny noses and fevers when everyone was wearing fabrics too thin to protect them from it.

His home was a tall, concrete building with a few dozen apartments. It had a comforting light blue facade and darker balconies framed by the red alder at the front. You'd think the blue would make it look cold, but somehow it never did. Cake really liked that shade of blue. The building to the left of it was orange and the one on the right was pinkish, both offsetting the blue in the middle in a pleasant way. Cake really rather liked the whole combination.

Every other window in the building had lights on, and cars were streaming past gently as people made their way home after a long day.

He stopped before the entrance and looked up.

Their lights were on. Matthew was already home.

Cake rented a decent size room in the apartment while Matthew was the main tenant. Technically, they were both paying the same amount of rent and had moved in together at the same time. He'd met Matt freshman year in college and they'd quickly realized that renting together was going to leave both of them more money to use, less time wasted on commuting, and less headache with dorm bathrooms.

Matthew had graduated two years ago.

Cake stared blindly at the pavement. He wasn't even looking at the ground. His belly might've been full and happy, but his mind was still trying to piece together a good working plan for what to do.

It was mostly coming up with a lot of nothing.

He ran his fingers through the sparse twigs of his beard and sighed.

A crow perched on a streetlight above him, and started pecking on the aluminum cover.

"Whatcha doing there, buddy?" Cake asked the crow. "You're not gonna get much out of that."

He stopped. The words hung in the low hum of the city and made his chest feel heavy. The crow tilted its head at him, then continued pecking. Cake stared at the bird, looking through its black feathers up into the sky as the beak sounded on the aluminum hood, clang clang clang a metronome to his thoughts of no money no job no time, and time slipping slipping fast and how was he going to spin this keep smiling it'll be ok. Then it stopped. The metallic clanging was gone and Cake snapped back into the moment. He turned to face the building. The crow was gone.

He trudged up the front steps.

Mac and cheese with truly extra sharp cheddar wafted from the kitchen.

"Hey! You cooking?!" Cake shouted from the door.

Matthew's head poked out from around the corner. "Hi... yeah. Trying on some cheeses," he waved the wrapper as proof.

"Smells good!" Cake put in extra effort to sound casual. On the bus he'd decided to not bring the work situation up just yet. He'd wait for a few days to see if his brain might manifest something. Money would've been nice but he didn't think his brain could do tricks like that. He'd settle for work or a general plan.

"Well, I hope so," Matthew smiled nervously. "Hey, I wanted to talk to you about something."

"Sure!"

Matt waited for Cake to make his way into the kitchen, then gestured at a seat.

"What's up? Whaddaya need help with?" Cake grinned.

"Uh..." Matt was rubbing his neck. "Ok, so this might be a bit sudden, but I think I might need you to move out."

Cake blinked. "Move... wait, you what MIGHT?"

"I mean, I do. I do need you to move out." Matt was rocking on his feet and stuffing his hands in his pockets so hard the stitching was snapping.

"Ok. Ok. How... what..." Cake was scrambling for words. "You want me to move out?"

"No no no," Matt leaned forward and put his hand on Cake's shoulder. "I don't WANT you to."

"But you need me to because of reasons unrelated to you? What the hell, man?"

"Jesus, I can't believe that disgusting meat eater has Coke Zero in his room. Like that's going to-..." Toni stopped dead on her tracks as she noticed the two men in the kitchen. She'd clearly been expecting less men and was only talking to one of them. Now there were two, which was one too many, and they were both staring at her.

She decided to stay perfectly still and silent in the hopes the situation might somehow change.

"She was in my room?" Cake looked back at Matt.

There was a brief, uncontested staring contest as Matt attempted a smile then remembered that it would've been inappropriate in the situation and just let out a half audible grunt and shrugged.

"She was in my room and that's all you have to say? About any of this!?" Cake bellowed standing up from the chair.

"I mean, I don't...," Matt kept spreading his hands and looking back at Toni who was sticking to playing possum, convinced no one had noticed her.

"What the actual hell is going on with the two of you?! I come home and the first thing you say is you want me out-..!"

"I don't WANT you out," Matt corrected him.

"I do!" Toni piped up.

"Well you would, you fucking kale wrap," Cake sneered.

"Hey now, that's out of order," Matt stepped in, beginning sternly then losing steam at around 'now' and ending with a compromising "Please don't talk to her like that, dude."

"I can go wherever the fuck I want in my own home, murder mouth!" Toni shouted back.

"Murder mouth.... Jesus, lady, you can't even insult people. And this isn't your home. This is my home!" Cake was waving his finger in Toni's face. "You're a fucking guest, so watch it or I'll plant you outside."

"You haven't told him yet?!" Toni turned to Matt.

"Told me..?" Cake cocked his head.

"Ah, what she'd trying to say," Matt had finally decided to stop digging a hole through his pockets, "is that we need you to move out because she'd moving in."

"There, I fucking told you. Loser." Toni crossed her arms and looked at Cake over her nose.

"Toni, could you give us a minute?" Matt glanced at her pointedly.

"What, you're gonna start telling me what to do now? What if I don't want to go?!" she sulked.

"Toni... please," Matt said with deep resignation in his voice. He'd lowered his hands to his hips and seemed to have aged about ten years in the span of the conversation.

"Fine." Toni spun around and stormed off to Matt's bedroom slamming the door behind her.

"I'm so gonna pay for that..." Matt shook his head, then looked up hoping for a sympathetic eye contact.

Cake had none to give.

"You fucker."

"Hey now. That's harsh," Matt pouted.

"I don't give a fuck and no, it's not harsh. This is my home! We're renting this together!"

"My name is on the lease, not yours." Matt noted.

"Really? You're really going to pull that shit," Cake guffawed. "You know it's only there because your daddy had the deposit to give."

"Ok, fine. Look..." Matt struggled which expression to leave on his face. "...Toni's periods are late."

A stunned silence fell over the kitchen as the men eyed each other; one looking for that chink to wedge open for sympathy and the other simply listening to the pasta water bubbling in the background with a sound that matched his brain's.

"So... her period is late," Cake shrugged finally. "You realize that means nothing. It just means her period is late. And now you're gonna start a family and kick out your friend?" Cake stared at Matt with the few pieces of respect he had left fast slipping away. "She's in a fucking cult! Fuck, maybe you two deserve each other," he threw his hand up. He was done. He was one hundred percent done with her and Matt and this godforsaken day and that cheddar was starting to stink like feet. Cake felt like he was stuck in a footlocker.

"It's not a cult!" Toni yelled from the bedroom.

"Toni, please! Let's just not-..."

"I don't give a fuck what you call yourself! Wearing robes and having secret handshakes and secret fucking smoothie recipes is a cult!" Cake was really starting to lose his temper.

"Children Of the Blessed Calm is not a goddamn cult, you murder mouth! This is what eating bacon does to your brain! You think living a little differently is like being in a cult!" Toni yelled through a cracked bedroom door.

"Come on, man. Don't talk to my girlfriend like that," Matt tried interjecting, still looking like a puppy that just ate a Rolex and was looking for sympathy because he was still hungry. He was looking for it from the wrong person.

"Jesus, she's three bricks short of a corner and you want to move in with her because that'll make a happy family? Fuck it. Fuck both of you,"

Cake grabbed his car keys from the side table and stormed out the door.

The door slammed shut behind him and he could feel the impact reverberate down his spine as he pounded down the hallway, down the stairs into the underground garage.

His Buick was sitting in its corner spot. He yanked the door open, got in and fastened the seat belt, skinning his thumb in the process. His hands were shaking. He stared furiously at the console, at the miles and the gas and the numbers moving and shifting in front of him while staying perfectly still. They didn't mean anything. They were just white blotches on a black canvas and he could feel the frustration building up behind his eyes, grabbing at the wheel until his knuckles were white and he couldn't feel his fingers. A clump in his throat was fighting to get out. It needed to get out, get away. His skin was tingling, failing the emotions under it. The lump inched up. Cake bent his head down. The lump lurched forward and was now on his tongue and oh god he couldn't hold these things anymore. Tears streamed down his face and he couldn't see and the lump was on his tongue making ugly sounds come out of his mouth so he let go and just let the tears flow.

After a while his skin stopped tingling.

When his eyes were starting to clear up, Cake let go of the steering wheel.

Maybe...

Maybe there was Norfolk. He could drive to Norfolk and sit at the look out and watch the city lights. Or call someone...

Cake turned the ignition. He looked at the numbers on the console again. They rearranged themselves, becoming miles and gallons once more. On his right the broken clock was blinking at 9pm. No, he couldn't drive to Norfolk, the gas was too low. And he needed gas to get to the old lady's place tomorrow and then for the drive to his mom's...

He turned off the ignition, then pulled out a phone while wiping his cheek on the back of his hand. The car felt surprisingly cold. He hadn't noticed the smell of gasoline before, or the vague smell of cigarettes he'd never smoked. The Buick's paint job was rusty on the outside and peeling around the headlights. The blue seats were ripped from corners and sagging in the middle.

Cake had never identified so strongly with a car before.

He pulled out his wallet from another pocket and picked out a black business card with silver inlays decorating both sides. After staring at the card for a while he turned it over and punched the numbers scribbled on the back in his phone.

The phone on the other end rang for a full minute. Cake checked his watch; It shouldn't be too late.

There was a click and a mechanical voice clattered: "You've reached the answering machine of doctor-..."

Cake hung up.

He leaned his forehead on the phone screen as the light from it faded leaving the car dark again. The garage lights turned off on cue, leaving the garage darker than a hermit crab's insides. It felt apt.

There was no sleeping in his own room tonight, Cake thought. He didn't have a room. He had stuff, and there was a room, but the room wasn't his anymore. Had it ever really been? He was just a placeholder for when the right Toni would show up with her tofu baby, and out he'd go because that's how much Matthew cared.

The car was his though.

Cake looked around.

The garage was starting to cool down as the night grew darker outside, and Cake realized he'd been sitting in his car for almost an hour, just staring ahead, his brain running on empty.

He looked at the back seat: connecting cables and a duffle bag with his running shoes. It would have to do for the night.

He climbed into the back seat and pulled out the complimentary t-shirt from his plastic bag. Thank god it was an XXL. Cake was a tall six foot something, but he wasn't very wide. He could comfortably wear a size small if the shirt cut let him.

He tried positioning the shirt as a blanket the best he could, pulling his long, gangly limbs closer in, and rolled the sneaker-bag up as a pillow. It was lumpy and uncomfortable and felt like shoes. The back seat was similarly lumpy. He felt vague shame for not vacuuming his car more often for situations like this, but then remembered that situations like this shouldn't happen, and the anger and frustration in his chest bubbled up again. Cake tried being angry until exhaustion gave away to restless sleep.

The night was very cold.

4.

It was a little past noon as Cake drove by the last house on the street. Miss Bannister's house was at the far end of the cul-de-sac. It was barely a cul-de-sac as there was almost an acre of empty grassland between her house and the nearest neighbors, and Miss Bannister's house stood alone at the very end of the street without a garage or much space to turn a car. The street just sort of stopped at her front door.

The last house before hers had a limp sign advertising "Turnop for president 2017" decorating an otherwise neat and minimalist yard. A small boy was crouched down behind the sign. He was playing with action figures, beating the dolls' heads together.

Cake cruised to a stop next to a red pickup truck in his beat up -92 Buick. The door made a sad creak as he got out. The car needed a check up and some new dampers. Cake's heart sank as he thought of the additional costs. He walked around the car kicking the tires; they seemed to be holding up even if they weren't looking like it. He decided to rotate them in the evening. Somewhere at a truck stop. His heart sunk further.

He didn't even want to think about everything that might be hanging by a hair under the hood.

The front porch was low and dim. Cake stomped up the steps in his pink khakis and a white tee like a man determined to get his hands dirty. The khakis really belonged to his brother, passed down through a few years of disuse, or whenever someone needed clothes that could get dirty. This usually meant Cake had them. Brutus had worn them once at a Pride and they'd gotten permanently stained with a multitude of colors. The pants had quickly gotten demoted to work clothes. But technically, they were still Brutus', as he would point out.

The house was immaculate but not exceptional. The gutters were clean and the front had a fresh paint job. There were small streaks of a dark paint on the very bottom corner of the door frame, but everything had a neatly uniform white and gray sheen to it.

The door opened before he had the chance to ring the doorbell.

"You're right on time, kid!" Miss Bannister squinted up at him. She was holding back two white goats wearing pajamas. One had bananas on it, the other owls. "Hold on a mo', I'll put these two ingrates in the basement and then I'll show you the lawnmower!" She slammed the door shut in Cake's face, and there was a brief silence. A short cacophony of swears and broken glass sounded through the door, before another silence.

The door opened again.

"To your left!" she marched past Cake waving her cane like a drill sergeant off to show some privates some ditches. "Your car!? Looks like a hearse!" she pointed as they passed the Buick.

"That's why I like it, ma'am," Cake attempted a friendly grin.

"Gertie! Everyone calls me Gertie!" Gertie quipped over her shoulder. "Even those Turnop fuckers over there!" She gestured over to the closest house with the sign on the front lawn. "Well, not the father! I think he calls me That Fucking Cunt!" Gertie chuckled.

"That's a nice truck you have there," Cake tried changing the subject as they passed around the side of the house to the back yard.

"It's my ex husband's!"

"Oh..," Cake started. "I figured you didn't get along with him much."

"I didn't!" Gertie waved her cane ahead of her. "There's the tool shed!" She pointed at a tiny, worn shed at the far end of what looked like yet another football field of empty space.

"You sure have a lot of space here." Cake ran his hand through his hair.

"Yeah! I bought the houses on either side and tore the ugly fuckers down! I don't need no damn peeping toms and their spawn running under my windows all day!" Gertie pulled open the shed door. It was barely the size of a portable toilet, with a loose light bulb hanging from the ceiling and a myriad of illegal wiring criss-crossing the wall next to the door. 'Wall' seemed like a charitable term to use in this context, Cake thought.

"There's the lawnmower!" Gertie pointed at a rusty little thing.

It was a push mower.

It was a push mower with sad, rusty blades turning over each other in a cylinder of brown despair and a set of ill-fitting wheels. One of them the original black and the other a dirty yellow half the size.

Cake fell silent. He could feel the wind drying out his open mouth. For 20 dollars.... His chest felt tight.

"Ha! I'm just fucking with you!" Gertie burst out. She pulled the covers from another lawnmower, this one with an engine and a shiny orange sheen. "Works every time! You kids always think I'm some old coot crazy enough to mow the entire 20 acres with a fucking push mower!" she giggled. "Hell no! Use this! Oh and there are some old shrubberies at the east side of my plot! They've been cut down already, but if you could be a doll and dig the roots out while you're there!" She pointed at a small shovel in the corner.

Cake sighed rubbing the back of his neck. "Sure thing, ma'am."

His chest didn't stop hurting.

He mowed the lawn.

And after that, Cake mowed more lawn.

The noon sun had long since peaked and was making its way into the evening streaking the sky with brilliant reds and oranges. Sparrows, robins and nightingales were chirping up a storm in the woods framing Miss Bannister's plot, digging and swooping after insects come out to play in the evening. Even with the lawnmower grumbling like a broken rhino in the grass, Cake could hear the discordant symphony of the birds. And beyond the woods, the steady hum of the interstate a few miles away.

By 6pm he was finally done with the mowing with just the single muddle of roots to pull out.

The sheared stump stood defiantly in the middle of the field. It was black and dead and definitely housing some sort of a bug infestation. Cake stood for a moment estimating the right angle to begin his approach as the tangled mess of roots poked out of the ground here and there creating almost a moat around the former shrub. Finally he spotted a good enough in and dug the shovel into the roots with his boot.

He twisted the shovel. The ground gave a cursory budge but the stump stayed put.

"Well shit..." Cake was wiping sweat from his brow.

He dug the shovel into a different spot and twisted again. The stump lifted and he could hear small roots snapping under the turf. But most of it remained unmoved.

"Really? After all this mowing? This is what you give me?" Cake gestured at the field. Irritated, he grabbed the little stump with his hands and almost immediately regretted the decision. The bark was dry and flaky and kept slipping in his palms. Whatever had built nests in the wood instantly went on the defense and he could see streams of black dots marching towards his hands from inside the stump, and the air getting darker as their aerial troops took flight. He squeezed tighter, rapidly blinking until he felt something lock between his hands and the wood. Cake dug in his heels and pulled. The dry bark disintegrated in his grasp and the remains of branches that had provided such a good grip dug into the sides of his palms. The harder he pulled, the deeper the withered remains pushed into his skin. It stung. Then it stopped stinging. The stump got firmer to grip as the blood from his hands wet the wood and the tiny roots kept snap snap snapping in almost a rhythm as he pulled and the mess of wood and blood and soil inched away from the earth until finally; a thick and satisfying pop. The stump, and Cake, flew back in an impressive arch, throwing earth up in the sky only for it to rain back down on him. Earth, stones, insects, and then larger white chunks that bounced off his arms and landed on the grass as he was trying to shield himself from the onslaught of soil.

Cake brushed his beard and sputtered bits of grit from between his lips. The white t-shirt was decidedly not white anymore with dirt and streaks of blood from his hand making a postmodern pattern on it.

"Oh, fuck me."

Cake looked down on himself as he got up. The skin on his hands was red and puckered up with blood seeping through, which was a small blessing. At least that would clean the wounds a little. He wondered if his tetanus shot was still effective. Had he gotten a tetanus shot?

He bent down to pick up the stump to drag it off to the composting heap when one of the larger chunks laying on the ground caught his eye.

It had a beak coming out of it.

Cake picked up the watermelon sized lump and turned it around. Yup, that was definitely a skull with a beak. A very large skull with a beak. Almost like a human crossed with Big Bird. A goth Big Bird. The cousin of Big Bird, who was actually into death metal and didn't like anyone on the Street except Oscar for shared bonding over garbage.

The eye sockets were huge and empty. The beak was a prominent outgrowth looking nothing like a nose, and very much like a beak. It had small serrated teeth-like things running along the edge of it. The back of the skull was a smooth creamy globe with barely visible light brown or yellow patterns, like animal tracks on a snowy field. But there was a very definitive jawline that pulled the bones into an oddly human-like shape.

Cake ran his hand over the skull, brushing away loose dirt still clinging to the nooks and the almost soft surface of the skull.

"Wonder if this is real."

He shook it upside down to see if there was anything inside it. Nothing seemed to rattle around and nothing fell out. The underside of the skull looked almost porous, like the edges of it had been burned with acid or decayed and the cell walls had worn thin exposing the empty cavities they were surrounding.

He sniffed it quickly.

It smelled of dirt and grass and gasoline.

Cake lifted the skull up to his face, brought it close and pinched his nose. He hesitated... then quickly pecked the skull with the tip of his tongue.

He stood still for a moment wondering what he was hoping to taste.

"I've been mowing this lawn WAY too damn long," he muttered to the skull. "Do you know what a skull tastes like? No, no you don't know what skull tastes like. What's wrong with you?"

Stumped, he kicked the grass only to hit what looked like a piece of a spine. A little further off from that, small femur-like bones and talons, scattered white splinters shining between the fresh grass. He picked up a few and turned them over in his hands. They looked the same: bones picked bare, some with corrosion exposing cell structures, mostly in shapes he couldn't identify. This was why paleontologist studied for many years, he figured, and he'd studied exactly zero years of How To Put Together Unidentified Bones.

"Whatcha got there, kid?!"

Gertie had somehow appeared behind him. Cake could've sworn she hadn't been anywhere near the side of the yard he was pulling roots from.

Then again, it was getting dark and Miss Bannister was very short, so she could've easily sneaked up on him through the undergrowth, he reasoned.

"Ah... uhm. I dunno. A really big bird?" he shoved the skull to the small woman in exchange for a can of lemonade.

"Where you get this?!" She stared at him unblinking over the skull. He tiny eyes seemed to glow in the settling dusk.

Cake pointed at the hole in the ground.

"I don't recall leaving this here!" Her eyes narrowed. She peeked into the hole as if to check if there were more of the same kind there. The darkness in the hole squirmed.

"That's some Halloween costume," Cake laughed nervously still holding the unopened lemonade can in his hand, the condensation soothing the angry welts in his palm pleasantly. The way the woman was staring at him though, felt much more unpleasant than the welts and there was no can of lemonade big enough to sooth that.

Gertie winked at him under her brow.

"Halloween. Yes! Right! Well done! Nicely shaved grass! Come along now!" She hobbled off towards the house with the skull tucked under her arm, waving her cane.

"But the... hole? Skull?" Cake hurried after her. The backyard was slowly filling with evening sounds again. He hadn't noticed how silents everything had gotten there for a moment. A cricket chirped hesitantly and soon birds were letting out their night calls in the distance, like the whole yard had held its breath until now.

"Yes! You've earned your twenty bucks! Good job!" Gertie shouted from her back porch while Cake was still lumbering after her a good 15 feet away. She was surprisingly fast for someone with the stride of a two-legged corgi.

"You did good!" Gertie blinked rapidly at the youth on her door step.

"Yeah, no biggie," Cake brushed his hair back then remembered his hand was still covered in dirt and blood and that was now in his hair too. He needed a shower. Then he remembered he couldn't take one at home because he didn't have one anymore.

A slightly awkward silence fell as reality briefly took hold of Cake's thoughts. Then he noticed a collection of eyes staring up at him from the darkness around the corner of the house. They all blinked out of sync.

"I like your cats," he said, nodding to the eyes.

"I don't have cats!"

"Uhm," Cake flustered. He looked back at the eyes in the dark and they were still there, staring at him, blinking whenever they felt like it.

"If you don't mind, you can probably take out the trash since you're going that way?!" Gertie kicked at two large black plastic bags next to her door. "My back's not what it used to be!" She grinned.

"Oh, sure-" The door slammed in his face. Cake folded the crisp 20 dollar bill into his pocket and grabbed the trash bags. They both weighed much more than he'd expected. He started pulling them off to the curb while digging his phone from his pocket with a free hand. A few messages from friends about a bowling night he'd completely forgotten. He thumbed a short rain check in the group chat. No missed calls. No mentions of him getting fired. Everyone had decided to collectively ignore it. He wondered how many had him blocked in the chat.

The trash bags plodded after him like they were filled with jelly and left a streak of wet on the asphalt. The street lights were slowly lighting up as moths, lacewings and mosquitoes started congregating under them. The sun had long since disappeared behind the horizon. Most of the other houses on the street were dark, with just a few windows at the other end lit up. The night was complete and serene.

Cake stopped at the curb. The Toters were full. He sighed and tried pushing the plastic bags as close to them as he could with his foot. The bags yielded then sprung back without having moved an inch. The jelly in them was slowly seeping out through the bottom.

"Fine, stay there," he stared at them angrily, then looked at his phone again. He flicked the Called Numbers up and picked the first one.

The phone rang like it was under water; a metallic, static, ear-bleeding ring that still felt like it came from inside a stuffed turkey.

"Doctor Duke's office, how may I help you?" a distant female voice answered.

"...office?"

"Yes. Doctor Duke's office. Can I help you?" the metallic woman repeated.

"No... no, I'm good. Thanks," Cake hung up. "Asshole," he sighed under his breath. A night wind suddenly rose up and blew goose bumps on his skin. The hair on his neck stood up as he looked around the empty and quiet cul-de-sac. The streetlight drew a friendly circle around him but outside it the front lawns looked just part of the shadows that had bled from the walls on to the ground. The houses were lumps of gray and the dark windows made it seem like no one lived there. Maybe no one did. Only the distant hum of the interstate and a faint salsa echoing from someone having a house party in a different part of the development reminded him of other people still being there. The phone in his hand felt comforting.

He thumbed it open again.

This time a warm female voice answered.

"Mom? Hey, you mind if I come over a day early? Yeah, nah, everything's cool. No, I'll tell you when I get there. I could just use an extra day of getting pampered by the world's best mom before a whole weekend with Brutus," Cake grinned at the phone. "Yeah, the key's in the same place? Cool. I'll start heading that way tonight. Alright, I'll see you then! Love you too, mom."

He stuffed the phone back in his pocket and traipsed to his car. After turning away from

the cul-de-sac and reaching the edge of the city
center, he stopped to drop off a thick envelope in
a collection box.

5.

Idaho Falls was just the right degree of warm this time of the ear. Not too hot and not yet deceptively cold. This time of the year, Idaho Falls was farms and woods and surprisingly modern homes with traditional pies and noodles without toppings. Come winter and it would be impenetrable roads, canned corn soup and competitive holiday light displays.

The sun was warming Cake's stiff fingers on the steering wheel as he pulled away from the Krispy Kreme with a box of fresh donuts on the seat next to him, and headed for Iona.

The car was quickly filling with the delicious smell.

He reached down to the cup holder and took a lingering sip from his coffee. He'd started for his mom's house the night before, after making a short stop at a state park parking lot. The night next to the lake was bitterly cool. Even after pulling on a woolly cardigan and getting his sleeping bag out from the trunk, it'd been a bit too much for him. He'd slept what he could, then got back in the driver's seat and took off for the nearest 24/7 gas station and tried warming up with a burger and the hand dryer in the men's room.

Cake pulled the sleeves of his cardigan over his knuckles.

The factory farms with thousands of cattle were sunning themselves in the late summer rays and Cake instinctively waved at the cows as he drove past them, then felt guilty like the cows might've taken it the wrong way. After all, he was going on a weekend getaway while they were going to be made into burgers. And he was going home to get pampered by his mother while they were separated early from their calves to produce milk. And the calves were probably all dead now too.

He felt a familiar lurch in his stomach as he'd managed to suitably bum himself out.

The radio kept blaring classic rock. There was a moment of silence after Stairway To Heaven ended for the dozenth time, then the square short plonks of Purple Haze started. Cake rushed to change the channel. He'd heard the piece at least six times on the drive already and had never really liked it. Now it was just plonking its way to his most hated list. Over the past few days he'd already learned that there was a surprisingly short list of songs that were considered "classic rock" and that stations were never allowed to deviate from the list, possibly under some threat of punishment. Excommunication from The Brotherhood of Classic Rock? Not a chance they would've played Gears of War soundtrack. He missed his Spotify playlists. The phone and the charger cable lay mangled on the seat next to him. He just felt tired to his bones.

After a little fiddling he found a station with local news and just let the newscaster babble in a monotone he couldn't quite hear over the AC.

The road was busy with 18-wheelers in red and white, carting cattle, feed, and dairy back and forth from the farms along the road. You could always see at least two or be sandwiched between them. Cake had a hard time keeping the Buick under control with his eyes feeling like very comfortable lead orbs inside his skull, weighing his head down as the pleasant sunshine warmed his body from the fingers up.

Two more miles, then I'm home, kept running through his mind. *Two more miles.*

He'd been psyching himself this way for the past 20 miles, but now it wasn't as much of a lie anymore.

The cattle in pens alongside the road blurred into a brown line between the green and the blue line and the forest on the other side of the road was a dark wall that blocked out the sky. It all seemed a little hazy to him. He focused on the fake wood dashboard of the car. How come he'd never realized before, how beautiful the paintwork on it was? They sure didn't make fake wood like that on discount cars like this anymore. You had to pay a fortune to get something like this... the light really was hitting the windshield wonderfully, reflecting off all the dust particles floating off the AC and the polyester seats.... Cake wished he had his camera to take some pictures. His eyes felt very heavy.

A truck whizzed past horns blaring and pulled him back to the road. He made a quick jerky correction only narrowly avoiding getting run over.

Two more miles.

The blue and white house he grew up in after they left New Port rose proudly between the trees. It wasn't a big house, but it had a house-like dignity that made it feel bigger than it was. The house had a low chain-link fence around it and two fancy but not too wide columns framing the front door, propping the raised canopy up. His mom was meticulous about keeping the house painted and the yard tidy. The lawn looked immaculate. Cake thought about mowing the lawn and shuddered.

There was a white dog house in the front and a row of petunias edging out the property.

The road was populated by houses for all different sizes of families. When they'd moved there, every single household had at least two children. Now the yards looked mostly empty of toys, and the number of potted plants had increased exponentially. The two car ports had remained as had the sense of community. Everyone was intrusive, but in the friendliest possible way.

Their house was on a corner lot. The house next to his mom's was a fancy white cement block with a gray cement garage and a pine jacuzzi at the back. The one on the opposite side of the street was a single level bungalow in dark browns, and two yellow-tinted windows facing the road. A narrow slate stone footpath ran alongside the driveway connecting all the houses. The area was designed for people who liked walking and cycling to the other end of the road, and for people who had small children and two cars which they didn't like mingling.

Cake pulled up in front of his mom's garage.

He stretched out his limbs getting out the car and let out a long yawn. An unkind whiff rose from his armpits. He pinched his nose. A shower would do good. He hadn't showered in two days now and had been living off gas station junk food, except for the block of cheese and the bag of toast he'd taken from the apartment when he left. He'd stayed in his car until he was sure both Toni and Matthew had left the place before going back and packing most of what he owned, anything important enough, in his car. It made him feel a little guilty. Matt and him had history. They'd been friends and roommates for over 5 years. At least he'd thought they'd been friends. Maybe that hadn't extended both ways. Maybe Matt always just saw him as an expendable piece of furniture. To be replaced with better furniture, furniture with boobs, once he had the money.

His expression grimmed. *Better not go there*.

Cake rubbed his eyes and saw Bob running to the fence to greet him.

Bob was a tubby little golden retriever. He was more like a barrel on two stumps than the kind of a dog you would see guarding houses. Cake's mom was convinced he might've had another breed mixed in, but it could just be that he was well fed and not blessed with long legs. When Bob wagged his tail, the entire dog would wiggle like a furry bowl of jello. Cake looked at the dog-butt going back and forth and it occurred to him that Bob never wagged his tail; he just moved his butt from side to side and the tail swooped after. He held his chin thoughtfully, then bent down to say hello back.

"Who's been a good boy?"

Bob wiggled as furiously as a fur-covered watermelon on a stick could.

"You are! Yes, you are a good boy!" Cake scratched the dog behind both ears and Bob flopped to the ground, rolling over in delight. Cake got on the ground next to him and rolled over too.

"Boy, I've missed you," he said, patting the dog's tummy. "You're such a stinky little lovebug."

Bob drew in a gargling breath, then hacked a ball of slime on the lawn and sneezed in Cake's face. He got up wiping his face on his sleeve.

"Maybe we talk to mom about your asthma medication?"

Bob wiggled excitedly.

The air was crisp. Cake stood with his eyes closed, just breathing in, letting the sun warm his body.

The clang of metal alerted him to the postman reaching for their mailbox.

"Oh hey, you can just give those to me!" He bounded over to the fence.

The postman stopped with one hand on the mailbox, the other holding a stack of letters. His expression was much like you'd expect from a startled postman.

"No."

"Come on, I'm just about to go in, I can just take those offa ya? It'll be easier?" Cake was looking up at the man radiating positive vibes the best he could, but also acutely aware of the funk emanating from his body.

"Are you Mr Johnson?" The postman said looking at the stack of mail in his hand.

"Sorta. I mean, I'm a mister and I'm a Johnson," Cake grinned brushing the back of his head. His strawberry blonde hair fell over his eyes. He pushed it back.

The postman remained unimpressed by the hair.

"No. This mail is for Ms Johnson, so I'm only allowed to release it to her care. Regulations. Aren't you a little young to be Mr Johnson?" he said arching a disapproving eyebrow.

"That's Janet's kid! Don't you sass him, Marvin!" a red headed woman from across the road yelled at them. She was wearing fluffy slippers and a green housecoat over her moomoo.

"Ma'am, I'm only following regulations! Official business. Please, do not interfere with a government official doing their job," the postman replied over his shoulder without loosening his grip on neither the mail nor the mailbox.

"Have you gone soft in the head, Marvin?! Stop being a dick to Cake! You've met him before!" the woman yelled back. Cake waved at her blushing slightly.

"Hi, Mrs Friday!"

It was nice that people remembered who you were, he thought, but it would also have been nice if people remembered you from something other than dressing up as an old naked man for Halloween when you were ten. The ten year old Cake had thought old naked person privates were the height of comedy, and had put a lot of time and effort into making his costume as anatomically correct as his adolescent brain thought it was. He'd gotten on first name terms that day with everyone in the neighborhood.

"Hey there, sweet cheeks!" She waved back. "Visiting mom, hu? Don't let Marvin walk all over you! He's been a dick to everyone since his wife left him!"

"Ma'am! You are interfering with the official business of a US government official. I'm afraid if you don't stand down, I'll have no choice but to write you up!" Marvin raised his voice. His dry white face and thin lips didn't seem to change their expression though. Rumor had had it he licked soup cans for fun.

Cake rubbed his brow.

"Look, I'm not looking to start any trouble here-..."

"What are you gonna do, Marvin? Hu?!" Mrs Friday shook her fist at them from her yard. "You gonna not deliver my bills? Ha! You can keep those!"

Cake sighed.

"I will report you to my superiors for proper reprimand protocols! Trust me, ma'am, you do not want to mess with the US Postal Service!" He turned back to eye Cake as the sole reason this whole interlude was taking place. Externally, Marvin did his best to look like he wasn't enjoying the idea. Internally he was struggling to contain himself; he might get to file a report. Mrs Friday was flipping him the bird. "You Civilians labor under the mistaken impression that following regulations is somehow 'wrong'. What would you do without regulations?" he whispered, leaning closer. "What would happen if we just started handing out mail to people willynilly on their say-so? Have you considered that? Of course not," he answered without waiting for a reply. "Rules are there to protect us all. Without them..." he leaned close enough for Cake to make out the dilated pores around his nose and the faint halitosis pushing out between the thin lips, "...chaos." The Postman remained staring down on him without blinking, much too close for comfort, until the natural unwashed musk of Cake's armpits reached him and he began blinking rapidly.

He stuffed the mail in the mailbox.

"Protect us from what... spam thieves...?" Cake muttered under his breath and opened the mail box. "This is okay though? I can take the mail *from* the box *after* you've put it in?"

The postman was already a few steps ahead on the foot path, digging his shoulder-bag. "It is out of my jurisdiction!"

"Jesus...," Cake mumbled flipping through the stack of letters. Mostly bills, and a few that looked like urgent bills but turned out to be junk mail disguised as bills. "Should probably burn these," he said to Bob taking out the junk mail into a separate pile from the rest. "You know she's gonna be too tired to notice they're not invoices..."

As he was sorting out the stack in his hand, Cake saw a blue Sedan pulling up into the driveway next to his car.

"Mom!" his entire face lit up as a tall, husky woman stepped out. Her hair was cut short and a little messy, with gray puffs here and there around the crown of her head. She pulled her gray, woolen jacket around her tight with a matching belt, and grinned back. A weight Cake hadn't even realized he was carrying evaporated as something warm and sunny flitted at the back of his mind. "You're home already?!"

"I wanna spend time with my baby boy!" the woman beamed pulling grocery bags out of the backseat of the car. She lifted up a jumbo tub of Ben&Jerry's. "I got ice cream! They got the big ones for once!"

"An' I got donuts!" Cake rushed to help her with the bags. Bob had already done his best to try and nab a bag with a brave little jump that hardly made it off the ground. The jump failing, he was content to thrash his backside from side to side.

They hugged hard.

"Oh my baby, how have... wow, you're ripe!" she pulled back half laughing. "Have you been sleeping in a dumpster? Has that vegan chick been cooking at your place again?"

"Nah, I just need a shower. Been mowing the lawn."

"Ok, alright," she raised an eyebrow behind her round glasses. "Well, I haven't touched your stuff, just moved some of my book boxes in there until I have the time to get them to the donation. All your," she waved her hand, "fancy tees and shorts are there if you wanna take a shower," she said with a pointed look. When his mom asked him things like these they were never really suggestions, more like orders softened up with the promise of ice cream and a friendlier reception if you followed them. If you failed to read between the lines though... Cake smiled a little stiffly.

"I really could use a shower," he agreed.

When Janet Johnson had been looking for a house for her two boys after the child support had actually started materializing, and they could afford to move away from the rapidly growing New Port, she had only a few requirements; everyone needed their own room. The boys were getting older and she wanted to have a place where she could lock the door on their running around to have time for herself. And it needed to have at least two full bathrooms, one for the master bedroom and one for the boys to share. She wasn't going to start arguing about taking too long in the bathroom with two teen-aged boys. And she wasn't going to start cleaning their messes once they reached the age where the messes became avoidable and not simple results of a child's uncoordinated limbs and boundless energy. She'd eventually found a house in the right price range that had two full bathrooms and a yard full of hogweed.

When Brutus was 10 and Cake was 8, she showed them how to clean every part of the bathroom and where the cleaning supplies were kept. There was a chart on the fridge they would have to mark when they'd done a full clean up. She would check. For a few years things went almost smoothly, with only a few clogged toilets. Then both of the boys had hit their teen-aged years and the bathroom cleaning routine had started deteriorating rapidly. She had talks, then lectures, then shouting. The cycle of unkempt bathroom hygiene might've never been broken unless both of them hadn't ended up at the doctor's with a mysterious ring-shaped rash on their buttocks. The doctor then lectured the blushing teens how the accumulation of bodily fluids and dead skin would very quickly start causing contact rashes and how everyone in the British Royal Navy in the 17th century was riddled with crotch lice and fungus because they couldn't wash their clothes or themselves properly while out in the sea.

The bathrooms had stayed clean ever since.

***

Cake stepped out of the shower pushing his hair back from his face. Showers were one of the miracles of the modern age. It washed away most things. Maybe not on a soul-level, but at least on a heart level. His body felt lighter and less like death. He looked down on his feet on the fresh bathroom mat and wiggled his toes. The mat had almost dried them already.

Brushing his back had pushed up the skin flaps in his palms he got from pulling out the stump from Miss Bannister's yard. Standing in front of the bathroom mirror, he looked at his palms; the little flaps were almost dry and dead enough to pull out but he didn't want to try now that the rest of his skin was so well hydrated. A small black dot was nestling between the ridges of his skin at the edge of the palm. It was a sliver of wood. He pursed his lips. *Damn wood. Damn splinters.* It was so close to the side of his hand it would've been easy to miss, as nothing Cake could think of would ever hit that particular spot. It could've stayed there and eventually turned his whole hand green if he didn't drop dead from blood poisoning before that. For the second time in as many days he wondered about his shots.

He took tweezers from the bathroom cabinet and went to the window to get a better look. The black sliver stood aggressively deep in

54

his skin, like a quill. He could almost feel the wood moving between his skin and his flesh when he pulled it out. The black dot was quickly replaced by a little red one.

Cake pecked the drop of blood off with his tongue, but it regenerated more quickly than it had appeared.

"Damn it," he sighed patting a band aid on the spot.

Putting the tweezers back he caught a glimpse of himself in the bathroom mirror. Mostly donuts and coffee wasn't much to build muscles on. He was tall with wide shoulders, but there wasn't much else there. He scratched under his chin pushing out the small stubble he'd managed to grow.

"Sheesh... pale."

Cake patted himself on the stomach and tried making his abs pop. The skin folded under strain but no muscles came to the surface.

He let out a deflated groan and started aggressively toweling himself off.

The towering book boxes formed a maze between the bathroom door and his closet. All the clothes he'd left there when he moved out the first time were still there. No books, no games. Those he took with him. Aside from the maze, his room was still the same as he'd left it. The clothes were also the same. Cake squinted at the rows of black and faded black shirts, heavy boots, pants with light weight chains hanging from them.

He settled on a gray t-shirt from the back of the closet he could've sworn was black. In the sunlight thought, it was definitely gray. It also had tiny, unintentional holes around the shoulder seams and a faded God Of War logo in the front. For the bottom half he was stuck between black cargo shorts that jingled gently when he moved and a pair of cut-off jean shorts.

He held both up, eyes darting from one to the other nervously.

"Hey there, nice turban!" Janet grinned as Cake finally sauntered into the kitchen with his hair wrapped in a towel.

"Heh..." Cake stared at his feet. The fluffy tiger slippers somehow still fit him. Then again, it'd only been four years since he last wore them. "Hair takes ages to dry these days." He adjusted the towel without thinking. It didn't need readjusting.

"You need a haircut, sweetie?"

"Nah, I'm growing it out. Can't tie it up yet," Cake said sitting down at the kitchen table and popping the doughnut box open. The jorts had been a surprisingly comfortable choice. They were almost too loose on him and didn't make a sound when Cake shuffled around in his slippers.

His bony knees were poking out from under the cut-offs like softballs in hot dog skins. Cake covered them with his hands.

The soft afterglow of freshness still radiated from the doughnuts as he stuffed them in his mouth. The frosting cracked with a faint sigh and the crispy outer layer of the doughnut crunched between his teeth as the soft middle yielded pleasantly. He closed his eyes enjoying the cornucopia of textures and flavors. His mother moved around the kitchen with short steps and loud dishes.

The kitchen had always been the heart of the house. More than the living room. More than their bedrooms. It was where everyone gathered after long days and where backpacks were flung against the wall and dirt from the garden and puddles was left after outdoor games. It was where hot cocoa was served after bad dates and where bills were secretly spread across the table on lonely nights. It was where you could always find everyone you needed at any given moment.

It had homely, off-white cabinet doors and tiled floors in dark slate. The counter tops were dark wood with worn edges and bumps where the brothers had hit their heads and elbows as their limbs grew out of their control. It wasn't a huge kitchen for growing boys, but it was big enough to fit a round pine table without blocking off escape routes from wedgies and nuggies. Around the table stood three green chairs. The fourth chair from the set was in the hallway next to the front door, carrying handbags, mail and small accessories. You could see to the living room from the wide doorway at one end. A broom closet was hidden away next to the table at the other. The quickest route from the boys' rooms to the kitchen table was from the doorway at the back. Cake's mom liked light colored place mats on the dining table even though everything looked a little yellow in the kitchen lighting, as the only window and the back door were on the shady side of the building.

Cake listened to the click click clicking of nails on tiles over boiling milk on the stove and the faint chattering on the TV. Bob sat down next to him and set his massive head on Cake's lap.

Huge brown eyes looked up at him expectantly.

"Hey, who's this?" Cake grinned down at him.

Bob blinked then burst out into a wide puppy smile.

"It's a good boy!" Cake ruffled his fur and loose skin. Bob drooled over his hands in delight. He held the dog's head in his hands, brushing the gray hair on the upper lip with his thumb, then ruffled the loose fur again.

"So how come you're home so early?" he asked as his mom was just putting the finishing whipped cream on two mugs of hot cocoa.

"Told ya, I wanna spend time with my baby. I hardly see you anymore," she set the mugs on the dining table.

"Mom, we facetime every weekend."

"It's not the same and you know it," Janet sat down with a plate of steaming, formerly frozen pizza already sliced up.

Bob huffed and flopped on to the floor, stretching a possessive paw over Cake's foot.

"Yeah, I guess it's not..."

"Anyway, I can take off. I'm senior staff, the residents got their meds and the kids can lift them on their own or call an ambulance without my supervision. I don't have to be there all the time," she continued picking up a slice and blowing on it. "Ok, tell me what's up," she beamed.

Cake stopped. Something was squeezing his stomach and it probably wasn't the doughnut. He hesitated.

Janet tilted her head. "Caa-ake...? What's up?" She held the pizza slice to the side.

"I got fired." Cake was avoiding eye contact.

A brief silence hung between them like a discreet ceiling fixture.

"You got fired. Okay. Well, that sucks."

"And Matthew is kicking me out."

Janet's brow furrowed. "He's kicking you out... now? Wait, why? Why would he suddenly just kick you out? You share rent!?"

Cake's lips were pressed together into a thin line. "He just... is," he made a waving motion. "He's starting a family. I guess. Toni is moving in. They're... having babies or something. I dunno." He let his hand fall down on his bare knee making a slap that startled Bob.

"He can't do that! You're both renting! Does he know you're fired?"

"I..." Cake spread his arms in a shrug. "I dunno. I guess. Maybe not? I didn't... I didn't tell him, no."

"Oh honey..."

"I didn't have the time, ok! I was busy! And anyway, it doesn't matter. I couldn't afford next month's rent anyway," Cake sulked into his cocoa. "It doesn't matter. I got kicked out of the internship and they're only gonna pay like a week's pay for the post stuff, which would be pennies anyway and they might not pay that and even if I got a lead on a new-..."

"Wait, why wouldn't they pay you?" Janet squinted. "It's your money, they legally have to pay you."

"Compensation," Cake glanced at his mom sideways quickly then moved on to Bob. "And maybe other stuff..."

"What did you do?" She leaned closer.

"Nothin'!"

"Cake Horatio Bartholomew Johnson. What did you do to them?" She was sounding out the words precisely, with a steady, slightly threatening tone she used when talking to rowdy pensioners.

Cake shrugged and tried patting the dog, but Bob ducked and gave him an accusing look. He sighed.

"I- I set their Roomba on fire. But that was an accident. Then the Roomba set the furniture on fire. That wasn't on me. But Mr Von Praeger probably thinks it is because it also burnt his favorite jacket..."

Janet's face was expressionless and her lips tight. She was still on the fence about this story. "But that's all covered under an insurance. I mean, if that jacket's so precious, he probably has a special clause for it, so it's not like he's losing money on this-"

"..and then I sent him a butt-scarf," Cake interjected into his hot chocolate.

"A what-now?"

"A scarf... with... a butt," Cake whispered, staring at Bob's big lumpy backside, and bracing himself. "My butt."

Bob also stared at his own butt. There was a silent bop and a noxious dog fart waffed over the kitchen.

Janet burst out laughing. "You sent him a scarf with your butt?! What? Why?! What is wrong with you?! How... do you have pictures?!" She was wiping away tears of laughter from her eyes.

"Uh, yeah," Cake dug out his phone. "This is the picture I used," he flipped open a picture of a pale pink butt crack covered in auburn hair with a puckered butt hole artfully centered in some rather flattering and artistic lighting.

Janet gasped and covered her mouth with her hands. "You did not. You did!" She looked at Cake. "My son! Is this how I raised you?" She stared at him intently then burst out laughing again.

Cake smirked awkwardly his shoulders dropping and a warm glimmer passing through him. Maybe this was going to be alright. Maybe he could figure this out. Mom was laughing.

Something grim whispered at the back of his mind.

"Oh my fucking god. Shoot. I mean, fudge. No fuck. Can't." Janet bit the inside of her cheek and tried steadying the corners of her mouth. Tears of laughter were streaming down her face.

"Oh my," she fanned herself huffing, trying to will gravity back into her face. "What did he say about your gift?" she managed in a professional tone, only her eyes completely betraying how not at all seriously she was taking this.

"I dunno. I just sent it off the day before. They haven't messaged me. Maybe he hasn't got it yet." Cake stared at the phone screen, then turned it off and laid the phone on the table. "I'm sure he's not gonna appreciate it like you do," he flashed a smile.

Janet glared at him, then guffawed and quickly covered her mouth with her hand again. She composed herself. "It's a very nicely lit image. But it probably cost you a fortune."

"Eh..." Tension creeped back into his shoulders. He didn't want to talk about money and this was headed towards talking about money. When you have none, it's the last thing you want to think about. He had none and he didn't want to think about it.

"So you're not going to graduate this year. That's not a big deal. But what's your money situation?" Janet leaned forward.

There it was. Cake pulled his head down like a turtle bracing for an impact.

"I have some."

"What's 'some'? How much do you have? How's your savings? "How big's the loan now?" She'd laid her hands on the table and was holding on to the side of it with one, like it was a raft.

"I've got, like, ten bucks..." Cake mumbled.

"How much?"

"I don't know exactly. At least fifteen bucks," he sat up straight in the chair and wondered why he'd lied. Five bucks wasn't going to make a difference one way or the other. "If the magazine decides to pay me anything and not withhold it for damages, it's still going to be only like a $150... something? Not enough for rent. Can't even imagine another semester," he crossed his hands on the table, leaving the quickly cooling cup of cocoa between his arms. The peaks in the whipped cream were melting and becoming dull mounds of semi-liquid cream. He quickly sipped from it to catch the fading warmth.

Janet tilted her head sympathetically. "Baby...."

"I mean, I gotta another job lined up end of next week, but-"

"Oh, so quick," she sat up straight with sincere admiration in her voice.

"Yeah, Talina hooked me up with this... er... place. It's ok. Uhm..." Cake rustled the hair at the back of his head. *Think fast, think on your feet.* "It's sales. Phone sales."

"Nothing wrong with that," Janet nodded approvingly.

"Weren't you the one who calls them pests?" Cake smirked.

"That's different. You're my son," Janet sipped from her mug. "And anyway, needs must when the devil honks or you know. It's not like a career or anything."

Cake's shoulders slumped. Not a career. This wasn't. What was his career?

Janet got up. "Oh hon." She hugged him tightly.

"Mom. Mom. Mom, I'm-..." Cake protested ineffectively before letting his hands drop and the hug take over. It was nice. His body relaxed into being a kid at home. Mom got his back. He was tiny and scrappy and always covered in burrs and snot as he came running into the kitchen again. The burrs dug into his glorious pouf of a hair and scratched his skin through the clothes. His tiny body was tense with pain spindling over his skin. Mom would rush over and blow on the scrapes, pull off the burrs and his eyes would stop hurting from the tears as she smiled down on him and pulled out a Batman band aid from somewhere. There were always band aids in her pockets. It hadn't occurred to him until now that she must've gotten up each morning and put a handful of them in the pocket of whatever she was wearing that day, and that was just part of her morning routine.

Cake looked up at his mom with a newfound admiration.

"You'll be alright. It's just another year," she smiled. He could see the tired lines around her mouth and eyes. "You're only 25. You got time. We'll ask around-"

...tonight on Oprah, special guest Doctor Duke!, the TV in the living room broke a perfectly lovely evening. They both glowered at the voice.

Janet stormed off to find the remote. "Oh for fuck's sake! How? How is this-," she angrily poked on the buttons of the remote, "Why is he on? Why?" She pointed at the screen.

Cake pinched the bridge of his nose. "I don't know, mom."

"Why would anyone want that... that glittery fucking charlatan on their show?! Jesus H!"

"Mom, calm down..."

"I can't have one evening to myself. Not. One. Without his face popping up everywhere. The women at the home," her arms flailed around dangerously, "they're all over him. Fucking cooing over that... that... pissing bag of goddamn fucking-" her hands landed on her head like they were trying to physically contain all her anger there, "shit eating permed garbage goblin!". She kicked a pillow lying between the sofa and the coffee table. The evening news theme tune filled the air and almost covered the sound of her grinding teeth. Her cheeks had flushed red and the muscles in her jawline were traveling down under the skin along with the anger.

"They weren't married to him, mom. How would they know?" Cake leaned his cheek on his hand. "It's ok. We can send him a scarf too."

Janet glared at him then burst out laughing. "Oh good lord, sweetie," she pulled the strings of her coat tighter and ambled back into the kitchen. Her face grew serious. "Have you tried asking him help with the..?" her hand made a flicking gesture.

"Nah."

"Maybe you should? He's your dad."

Cake stuffed two marshmallows in his cheeks. "Camf noft. Amf a chipfmunkh nowf."

6

"No," Janet held her finger up while continuing to rinse the dishes with her other hand.

"But it's just-"

"No. You take that outside," she pointed at the door.

Brutus grabbed his phone from the table and mumbled something unintelligible through the vape pen as he got up.

"Wait," Janet put the last plate on the rack next to the sink and watched intently as the soapy water swirled down the drain. She weighed the fresh air in her lungs for a moment. Brutus was frozen in place in a half-twist. "Come," Janet motioned him to come over. He complied. She wiped her hands with a small cotton towel then plucked the e-cigarette he was holding from his hand and took a drag from it.

She held her breath. Opaque puffs of smoke tried escaping her nostrils but she willed them back in. Then she quickly turned to the now empty sink, and blew the smoke into the garbage disposal.

"I don't think that does anything," Brutus remarked, his voice tight with irritation. Their roles in the family hierarchy would never shift; she was The Mother and she would always have a mother's command over who smoked what in her house. She would do things she told him not to and tell him what kind of shoes to wear in family events. And she could do all that without saying a word.

Janet grimaced. "Jesus, what do you put in that thing? That's not tobacco. Can't be weed unless you grew it in a cologne bottle,"

"It's my own blend," Brutus said indignantly.

She looked at him over her glasses.

"Premium cigar with a dash of orange peel."

Janet frowned as she tilted her head.

"I like it." Brutus nabbed the gadget back and turned on his heel. He slammed the door behind him a little too hard for Janet's liking.

Cake set his empty coffee mug on the kitchen counter and shared a meaningful glance with his mother. She rolled her eyes then grinned.

"He doesn't mean it," Cake tried.

"Oh of course he does. I'm his mother, he's my baby. It pisses him off that that's just how it is and that I give him shit about his whiney-ass Turnop-buddies. He's my big, obnoxious baby and I love him, but you know he has poor taste in everything," she waved her hand. "I just hope you two have a good time," she reached over to give Cake a hug.

Janet was much smaller now that they were both standing up. Her face barely reached Cake's collar bones. He rested his cheek on her head. Did she shrink overnight? Brutus was puffing thick clouds of vapor right next to the window and the bitter orange scent drifted in. It really did smell like rotten sanitary towels, Cake thought.

"Let's go, jughead!" Brutus shouted from the other side of the car.

"Hey, keys! I can put your car in the garage..." Janet shouted from the porch.

Cake bounded back up the stairs in one leap and handed her the keys. "Thanks, mom. Don't worry about the stuff in the back, I'll take-,"

She waved him off so Cake just nodded and bounced back down the lawn to the waiting car.

"Don't set anything on fire!" Janet waved at them as Cake climbed on the passenger seat of Brutus's custom copper-tone Land Cruiser.

"We won't. I won't! Not making promises for skidmark!"

Cake frowned at Brutus as he settled into the driver's seat.

"What?"

"Rich coming from a smoker."

Brutus smirked and backed the car out of the driveway. They were off.

The suburban houses quickly made way for potato fields dotted by a farm house here and there. The woods were an ever looming dark belt between the sky and the crops with a soundtrack of 1980s glam rock Brutus liked humming along to, as the car floated along the highway. The car was fresh. Cake remembered it being green the last time he saw it, but then again, the console had also been filled with actual buttons instead of touch screens, so he decided it was probably a different car.

He leaned his forehead against the side window and let the scenery blur with the hum of the road into an uneasy lullaby. Brutus kept belting to Mott The Hoople in the driver's seat.

Cake drifted off. Up, off with the sunshine and the full belly and the familiar but new scent of the car. The cars always smelled the same on camping trips. Different people, different cars. Always the same camping trip smell. Except for that one time with the fish. They thought it was a good idea to take home the fish they'd caught instead of eating it there at the park like they usually did. Cake, Brutus, mom and dad. The car didn't smell the same then. The rubber boots, the fresh bait jar and a hook with a worm on it. Their dad in his hip-high boots standing in the creek. He could catch fish. He was the fish master. That's what he said. The day was bright and the surface of the water reflected a myriad little bugs tempting their fate over it. Dad was going to catch fish. He pulled out tiny little minnows, one after the other and by the sixth his face was deep red and a vein was bulging in his forehead and he let out words Cake had never heard. The fishing rod shook in his hand as he climbed out of the stream. Cake saw his own round face reflected in dad's mirror shades as he barreled past. Brutus was standing a little further off in the stream, pulling up something big from the water. Cake looked down on the bait jar with the earthworms toiling away in dirt. He poked at them. The worms were squishy and pleasant and scrunched up under his finger. Dad was shouting at them to get in the van and now Cake was sitting next to Brutus looking at the blue sky through a window as Hoople had changed to Slade.

"You ok there, bro?"

"Yeah, just thinking about the stinky fish," Cake grinned. "When did you get the new wheels?"

"Oh, you noticed," Brutus looked very pleased with himself. "Just got it like, 2 months ago. I think? You like?"

"It's really nice. Roomy. Good for sleeping in."

Brutus gave him a sideways glance.

"I mean, hypothetically, if someone needed to sleep in a car, this would be a good car to sleep in," Cake continued.

"...Sure. Or they could just sleep in their bed. Hypothetically."

"Not everyone has a bed," Cake turned back to look at the sky.

"Oh come on, bro." Brutus let out an exasperate groan. "You fucken' have a bed. You got two!"

Cake pulled his head between his shoulders. "It's not about that..."

"Then what?! Goddamn you have a bed and you went off and slept in your car like some fucking hobo just because you couldn't stand up for yerself and now you're all sulky 'cuz you need to find new digs? Jesus, stop whining!"

"What? What should've I done? Beat the crap out of Matt? Is that your solution to everything?"

"How.. how did you even get from standing up for yourself to beating his shitty, double-crossing ass? I mean, I'm not opposed to it...," Brutus rubbed his forehead with his free hand then rolled the side window down and leaned his elbow out. "I mean, just grow some damn balls and tell the motherfucker to stay the fuck out of your room and you'll move when you fucking like it."

Cake stared out into the wide empty plains through the window. "I don't think that's how friendships work."

"Well, he wasn't much of a friend. Like-.."

"... I'm not sure I even know what I'm doing anymore," Cake mumbled to the side window.

"Fuck, you shoulda just gone to IT. Who even studies photography? No one cares. No one," Brutus eyed him up with his brows knit together.

"Cuz we all just need to go to IT and make sponsor deals with the Dew? I'm not you, bro. I don't care about computers."

"You use Lightbox though. And sell your stuff online. That's like saying you don't care about air."

"Yeah, but it's not like that! You think everyone in the world should just go to IT cuz that's where the jobs are? Sure, let's just not eat anymore. Fuck food, right? IT is where it's at!" Cake waved his hand over the dashboard.

"Dude, you need to get laid."

Cake buried his face in his hands and let out a muffled groan. "Could you just for once get that I don't do that?" He raised his face from his hands curling his fingers into fists because this was a conversation he'd had too many times before. Every time he was anxious or tired or just hungry, someone would bring out the 'just get laid'. And when he said no, they'd go down the same route...

"Can't you just get on hormones or something? That shit ain't natural," Brutus glared at him from the corner of his eye.

That route. The same one every time. That there was something wrong with not wanting to get laid.

"Fuck off. Every time. Every single time," Cake squeezed his fists trying to temper the anger prickling his chest and back.

"There's no such thing as an asexual, bro. You need to get your damn soy-hormones checked."

"Yeah, I've just been ace since... I dunno, birth. Go on, keep telling me I'm not real. This is really fucking helpful." He was holding his eyes closed as the hot rattling anger vibrated up his neck.

"What, you gonna get up on me about this shit again? Christ!" The car broke to a screeching halt on the side of the road. Cake had to brace himself as the dashboard suddenly rushed towards him.

"What the hell are you doing?!"

Brutus was climbing out of the driver's side. "You're driving!" he shouted over the bonnet. "Get out, you're taking the fucking wheel," he pulled the passenger side door open and Cake clambered out confused. "I'm too fucking sober to deal with you all weekend."

They switched seats and the car curved back the road, Cake nervously checking the sides trying to catch up with the weirdly smooth dashboard and feel of the car. Brutus leaned over to the back seat and pulled out a can of beer. He downed it in one, then reached for another. After another half a can, he exhaled a little of the tension and let it be sucked out through the open side window. Cake was hunched over the steering wheel like a rabbit, tensing every non-existing muscle in his body as he tried to remember how SUVs worked.

"Bro, it's not that deep," Brutus said to the dashboard, rubbing the beer can on his forehead. The cool of it had condensed into water immediately and left a wet streak across his head. Cake glanced over and bit the inside of his cheek to muffle a laugh. "What?"

"You got... you got a little something," he wiggled his index finger around his forehead, "...uh, glow?"

"Shit!" Brutus sat up and rubbed his face furiously on his t-shirt. "Jesus, just hanging out with you spreads the loser vibes."

"Yes," Cake stared at him deadpan. "This is all my fault."

The rest of the tension evaporated into the AC. Shoulders dropped. The smell of micro-brewed cocoa beer slowly filled the car as T.Rex announced they should feel the noise on the radio.

Cake found himself tapping along on the steering wheel and when the chorus line hit, they both joined in, singing spectacularly off-key. Neither ever had a talent for anything but listening to music. But that never stopped them, to the misfortune of everyone around.

The last plucks of the guitar melted into the highway and something else picked up their place.

"So how's Marco?"

Brutus blushed. When he blushed it was a magnificent display of scarlet running down to his hands, like a reverse peacock spreading its tail. If the tail was red instead of green. And the peacock was a bear instead of a bird.

Cake sniggered.

"… gonna… him… rry…," Brutus mumbled, the red swallowing his hairline and sideburns making his head look like a pot roast.

"What? Can't hear you!"

"I'm gonna ask him to marry me, ok!" Brutus spat out almost angrily.

"Oh wow. Now was that so hard?" Cake chuckled. "When? What's the date? Have you got a ring yet? Oh man, my big brother's gonna be a married man!" The sky was now so intensely blue,

Cake could feel his heart drowning in it. There was gonna be a wedding. He'd get to be a best man.

"Yeah... yeah. I mean, I got one on order. Gotta pick it up next week." Brutus dug out his phone and flicked it around to find a picture. "Here," he shoved the phone at Cake.

The ring was a black and white, two tone band with two thin platinum stripes and a black titanium stripe running between them. The platinum stripes had some sort of texture on them, which Cake couldn't make out while staying on the road at the same time.

"That's pretty impressive," he breathed. It was. He was genuinely impressed by the simple design. With all his obsession over electronic gadgets, Brutus had an uneven taste in design. It was either terrible or wonderful, with a heavy lean on really fucking awful most of the time. "When you gonna ask him?"

Brutus scowled at the windshield and Cake could see his jawline moving under his stubble as he ground his back teeth.

"You don't know yet, do ya?" He turned back to the road with a little smirk. Brutus was bad at not knowing. He had to know, he had to have the right answers and if he didn't, he was likely to get sulky, like the brief moments of indecision were ugly shoes he had to wear to church. "...want suggestions?" Cake tried.

"Look, it has to be perfect!" Brutus snarled, rubbing his forehead, then swigging back the last of his second can. He stared at the can with mild disappointment lost in thoughts that included private trips to microbreweries or possibly that tacky water park Marco liked and he could barely tolerate. "I'll buy him a dolphin…," he muttered.

"Aaaaww!" Cake let out, then quickly straightened up, "wait, can you do that? I mean, are people allowed to have dolphins?"

"Who cares? I'll get him a dolphin and feed the ring to it and then serve the dolphin as dinner," Brutus said at the empty can.

Cake stared at his brother for a moment, trying to remember if their dad had been this way. He only remembered the angry bulging veins on his neck and forehead and the gentleman's hats he wore to cover the blond curls retreating over the top of his head. Even his hair had been afraid of those veins.

"Did you call dad?" Brutus changed the subject.

"Uh.. yeah."

"He didn't have leads for ya?"

"I got his office. Some secretary answered." Something small and heavy made it's way to Cake's heart and was now kicking the walls from the inside.

"Oh," Brutus returned to his third beer. "He probably just sent the wrong business card."

"Yeah…" A kick struck him in the rib. From the corner of his eyes, Cake saw Brutus relaxing in the seat, nursing the sweet smelling can, content that everything was resolved. The world was at peace and he knew all the right answers.

Cake wondered what that must've felt like.

The evening sky was a glorious show of pinks and golds and the beer seemed infinite. Half way through his fourth, Cake started wondering where all the cans were coming from. If the new car was, in fact, hollow and filled with beer. Then Brutus wandered over and stuffed a hot s'more in his mouth, humming something that was probably a mix of all of the songs, and made a toast.

"Toast to the best brother! And the wood gods! Valhalla!" he necked another can and Cake had no idea how many this was as the world was now entirely made of beer and bonfires and the best dance moves he'd ever made as Brutus cranked up the radio.

The world swung gently around them catching on to the music as he stumbled over to Brutus and draped himself over him: "Best brother..." he slurred.

"Death and glory!" Brutus bellowed, smashing a can to the ground and stomping on it. "We're gonna get tattoos! Matching tattoos!"

Cake felt something faint at the back of his mind as a reasonable thought tried pushing through but beer quickly sloshed over it. "Nah..." he giggled to himself.

"Dicks! Two dicks! The Johnson brothers!" Brutus swung his arms around. "We're gonna ruin that perfect skin of yours." He burst out laughing.

"Brutus, no..."

"Brutus yes!" He made a small pirouette belly first, making Cake lose his balance and plop down on his backside. "Oh, I need to pee. In the tent!" Brutus wobbled off to the tent.

Cake swayed bemused on the ground for a moment, before noticing the cooler. He dragged himself over and rummaged around keeping one eye closed as he felt it helped with his aim, and finally found a pack of hot dogs. He tore into it with his teeth and chewed on the plastic staring at the bonfire. The radio was steadily getting more silent as the battery ran down and Cake soon got tired of the plastic, spitting it out. He dug into the contents of the package and never in his life had cold dogs tasted so good. He stuck one on a stick after only a few tries, then stuck it directly into the fire. As the skin of the sausage cracked and purled open, a quiet snoring rose from their tent.

A few sausages later Cake felt the soft buzz of the beer lulling around at the edges of his consciousness, pulling sleep in closer. He was cozy enough in the sleeping bag but worries kept poking their head up in his mind like worms in a bait jar. He couldn't stop jabbing at them. The more the beer wore off, the more aggressive the worries got, squirming their way brazenly across his sleepy brain. Wild crickets were a muffled white noise outside the tent and Brutus had fallen asleep the moment he'd put his head down, but life was keeping Cake awake.

He stared at the of top the tent; the poles holding it up made a barely visible cross on the roof and he thought he could see a meaning there, thought of course they were just poles and had no answers to give. His mind was wading in the witching hour, not even sure if it was night anymore, if he was awake of asleep. All he could see was that cross on top of him.

From the edges of sleep came a buzz. A mosquito. There was a mosquito in the tent. The buzzing came in and out of ear shot. Cake pulled the sleeping bag closed tighter so only his face was visible from the polyester tube. He laid motionless, pretending to be a gigantic nylon grub. The buzzing persisted. Then a bright light lit up right over his face.

It wasn't a mosquito after all.

Just a lightning bug.

Cake let out a sigh and his whole grub body relaxed. The little light twinkled on and off hovering over him. For some reason it made him feel happy. That little magic in a very ordinary world.

The bug changed color.

As it hovered, it slowly shifted from bright white to green, then purple, then red. It stayed almost unnaturally still now, changing its colors and humming like nothing at all he'd seen before. Cake's eyes narrowed. This was new for lightning bugs. Maybe they'd evolved to compete with the rest stop signs. Maybe they'd eaten GMO crops. But this was definitely new. The bug made a tiny circle then flew off and he could hear the tiniest thud on the tent fabric. It reappeared glowing purple, then green and then disappeared again. There was a tiny thud.

"What're you doing, lil' bug fella? You trynna get out?" Cake slurred half asleep.

The bug reappeared shifting from blue to red making a slightly louder buzzing sound. Then it flew off in a huff and there were two consecutive thuds on the tent.

"Bro, are you seeing this?" Cake tried nudging Brutus. "We got a magic bug. Am I asleep?"

"… yes… you asleep. Go back to sleep," Brutus mumbled from inside his sleeping bag without moving.

Cake glanced over, then back at the bug bumping heroically against the tent fabric, changing its color now more quickly.

"You want out? Now? Ok, lil' guy, I'll let you out even if you're gonna get a lot of mosquitoes inside." He unzipped his cocoon and fumbled over to the tent door surprised how the beer had made the air warmer or his skin hotter. He couldn't decide which.

The lightning bug slipped out of the tent as soon as he'd zipped the door open all the way, and as the fabric fell back from the opening he could see the entire forest full of lights, twinkling in different colors. Little starts covering the ground and bushes, illuminating the tree trunks in peculiar detail, pulsing and humming in anticipation.

Cake's mouth dropped open.

He climbed out on his hands and knees following the tent bug and the lights covering the darkness drew closer.

"Holy wow. There's a lot of you," he breathed.

The lights circled him then formed a brilliant, thick ring in the air in front of him as the lone tent bug flew through the circle. Cake reached out and tried touching the side of the ring, but his fingers fell through it, only touching air and wisps of wings. The ring reassembled itself where he'd disturbed it. A wave of color went around it as the bugs changed shades in unison. An electric hum had filled the woods and he hadn't even noticed that the sound of crickets had died down as he wondered at the glowing circle floating in front of him. As quickly as they'd flocked into one shape, the bugs dispersed and formed an arrow pointing to the woods.

Cake squinted.

"You... you want me to go there?" he pointed in the arrow's direction perfectly aware that he was now really talking to lightning bugs and not just mumbling theoretical questions to himself.

A pulse of color rippled through the arrow in the direction it was pointing.

"You want me to go that way," Cake repeated feeling assured. "Ok, sure. I mean, I'm dreaming so let's go that way."

The arrow dispersed to form a line of fading stars leading into the woods. Cake pulled on his shoes and stumbled along it into the darkness mildly annoyed at himself how he had to put on shoes in a dream and couldn't just imagine them on like a normal person.

After a few minutes of walking, propelled by the gentle fuzz of beer, trying to focus on the lights in the perfect darkness that was the state park night without neon signs or street lights, the trail of lightning bugs ended near a rocky ford, where the river water pooled into different sized ponds as it flowed over and continued on to a cascade. Most of the pools weren't very deep, bowls and vases, bucket-sized at the most, but a few were the size of a hot tub. It was one of those natural hot tubs the shiny bugs pointed towards. As Cake got to the end of their path, a cloud of lights rushed over him, circling the pond.

"You guys sure are well organized."

The little bugs twirled over the water. They formed another arrow pulsing in different shades towards the pool, then dove in. The arrow sunk in the water along with the electric hum and left the night completely silent.

"Hey!" Cake ran to the pool. There was a faint glow coming from under the black water. He stood there with his hands on his hips staring at the deep. "You just gonna leave me here?"

A single lightning bug emerged from the water and floated in front of him for a second, then it plunged back into the dark.

"Ok, so what I'm getting here is you want me to take a swim?" Cake pursed his lips. The little light rose again from the water, only a few inches above it this time, then sunk back in. "Ok, fine, just hold on," Cake said pulling off his clothes. Again he was silently annoyed that his dream wouldn't let him skip to the part where he was already naked and taking a bath. He folded his clothes neatly on a dry rock and set his shoes next to them before carefully taking a first step into the water. This wasn't the first time he'd been here. He'd soaked his feet in these pools when he was a kid, but somehow camping trips with Brutus were always more about beer and 'smores and less about getting your feet wet.

He was hip deep now and the water was still feeling very pleasant seasonal factors considered. What he would have cared for if he was more sober and this wasn't a dream, was that he couldn't see the bottom and the pool was probably filled with squirrel and bird droppings, but as those things didn't matter in a dream he waded in deeper. The pool had natural rock 'stairs' on one side but there was really no telling how deep it could suddenly get after those ended.

Cake peered down to see the faint lights swirling in the endless night mixing in with the reflection of the stars above, and himself in the between, a slender silhouette.

"All the way down?" he asked the water.

The lonely lightning bug reemerged, then dove back down again.

"I'll take that as a yes," Cake said and took another step. The stairs ended and his feet landed on nothing. It was a surprisingly deep pool, he thought idly as the water closed over him.

7.

Early morning sun fell gently through the mist the night had brought. It skipped over waters and warmed rocks and invited birds from their resting places to sign its praises. Bit by bit, the air would warm to its embrace, and summer blossom to full glory. By noon, the rocks would be hot enough to fry an egg and all the myriad little lizards normally enjoying the undersides of rocks would be tanning their hides on top of them.

The pool was warm like mother's milk as Cake stood up. It was the only expression that came to his mind describing how lovely the water felt but he'd never actually swam in breast milk, so it felt odd and a little invasive to him to describe nice baths that way. He resolved to find another expression for a pleasant warmth by the end of the day.

The water trailed smoothly along his wide shoulders and abs, seeking to join in lows rather than highs. A few gathered between the bulges of his abs and nestled in his belly button. He slowly waded to the edge of the pool and climbed out. The lasts wisps of mist twirled around his ankles as he closed his eyes and listened to a cuckoo song echoing over the river. It was a beautiful morning.

85

Cake stretched out and looked around as the sun continued to warm his body. He left his clothes here. He was sure he had put them in a stack on that rock. But the rock was bare. No clothes. And no shoes.

Brutus. Damn it.

He pursed his lips tight looking at his prosthesis; swimming with the full toe prosthetic had been a bad idea. Now it was wet and there was water between it and his foot. He sat down on his bare butt to take it off and let his foot air out. The elastic sole separating from his real foot produced a satisfying plop and scared a bird from the treeline on the other side. Cake grinned after it as the flapping of the wings echoed from the trees and the rocks.

Early mornings were always so quiet. Like the world was standing still. Cake breathed in deeply of the crisp morning air. It was going to be a great day.

He made his way carefully over the rocky ford to the treeline with the prosthetic in his hand. His soles quickly adjusted to how the bare ground poked and cooled them and his gait got easier. The forest between the river and their camping spot looked so much sparser in daylight. Every shrub and fir needle was clearly defined. Cake traipsed along confidently. With this much light, he could see any snakes coming a mile away. Or at least a feet or two, he thought, as long as he looked at the ground. They did move rather low. He slowed down and stepped more precisely.

There was, in fact, a faint footpath between the opening and the river and he tried footing along the even ground without straying too much on the moss and sprigs. Something large took off to the right of him and disappeared too fast for Cake to catch if it was a deer or something else. He stopped to stare after it into the deep green. An echo of leaves rustling followed from further off but nothing else. He stood perfectly still for a moment, holding his breath. Nothing.

As he turned back to the path, an unnaturally yellow blotch caught his eye.

There was a piece of tape tied around a tree. It looked like it might've been there for a while, he thought, pulling at the plastic between his fingers, then rubbing the dust off on his thigh. It left a dark gray streak. Cake pouted at it disapprovingly, then bent down and wiped his hand on some suitably moist-looking moss. The camping ground was just a few steps ahead, but...

Brutus' car was gone. So was his tent. And his and his sleeping bags and travel radio and portable cooler and the beer and the hot dogs and the little folding chairs. Cake also saw no clothes anywhere.

This was starting to go a little too far.

He puckered his lips tighter and started off in the direction of the park rangers cabin in a huff. The morning air was making his hair stand on end and starting to feel unpleasantly cold on his privates. Almost any other part of his body was perfectly fine with the occasional airing, but a man's privates were his privates and he wasn't happy about having to air them out involuntarily. A gust of gentle wind traveled up his butt crack in a way that made him instinctively clench.

The road from the gate to their camping spot was luckily paved. It was warming up nicely as Cake steamed along, thinking of his choice words to Brutus. If he thought making his newly destitute brother walk naked all the way to the entrance of the park - a good hour and half of walking - was a funny prank, Cake had opinions. They weren't brotherly opinions. They involved putting Nair in his shampoo or drawing vaginas on Brutus' face while he slept. The opinions also included some gentle punching in the face.

He ran out of stomping speed about half an hour in.

Another ten minutes of annoyed walking, and the paved road curved in two; one road leading to the main gate, the other to a parking lot fenced by rental cabins.

Cake and Brutus never took those. Their dad had insisted that rented cabins were for useless city folk who couldn't fend for themselves in the wild. "Real men use tents!" he'd raged while they drove past, an hour before he threw the fishing rod into the woods and told the boys to get back into the car with their stinky fish. He'd never taken them camping again, but texted them pictures of very large fish from a farmer's market. Cake was never sure if his dad's attraction to the wild was more about the wild as an allegory for his receding hairline and rapidly disappearing upper body strength, or about his obsessive attraction to fish.

Other people had less issues with using cabins though. Other people might also have clothes and cars.

Cake took a left for the cabins.

The log cabins looked quiet and Cake instinctively reached for his phone to check for time. His phone wasn't there, because his pockets weren't there. He let out an irritated huff.

The cars in front of the cabins stood immobile and as dark as the cabins.

There didn't seem to be any movement even though morning was generally the time when people who came here to fish, would pack up and drive further off to the flats for morning bait. He stood in the crossroads for a second considering his nakedness. His stomach growled. At the very least they might offer him something to drink. Hopefully from a glass or a bottle.

Standing naked in front of the first cabin's door with a fake foot in his hand, Cake's heart squeezed a little. They might scream. They could also point a gun at him. His stomach growled louder.

His knocking echoed softly through the wooden door as Cake waited holding his breath tighter than his foot.

Not a peep.

He knocked again. And again.

Nothing.

Undeterred, he moved to the next cabin door and did the same. Still nothing. Nothing but his breathing and the uncomfortable pounding of his heart as he tried to listen for any signs of movement.

"Hellooo-o! Is anyone in there?"

The door didn't answer.

He glanced at the blue hatchback in front of the cabin with an army green tarp covering whatever was on top of it. A far end corner flapped around in the breeze.

Cake moved on to the next cabin and noticed a group of deer lazily making their way across the parking lot. They stopped to stare at him, then sniffed the air and examined the asphalt. *Nothing but local deer being deer*, Cake thought as he turned to knock on yet another cabin door. A silence flowed from the cabin, punctuated by the deer hooves etching, clicking, closer. They were examining the blue hatchback now, leaving long snotty marks around the sides in the condensation. One of them chewed on the tarp nonchalantly.

"Hey!" Cake took a step forward. "Hey! Stop doing that! That's not deer food!" he shook his prosthesis at the deer.

They stopped with ears perched to receive.

"Shoo, you lunatics!" He took another step forward trying to look intimidating with his arms raised above his head, and managing a very convincing flap as his bare foot slapped against the cabin porch. The deer jumped.

"Shoo!" he waved both arms menacingly and the deer took off running into the thicket. "Damn wildlife…," Cake muttered. "You could've died, you idiots! That's not for deer! It ain't food, you dumbasses, you're fucking welcome!" he shouted after them, then turned back to the door.

It stood unchanged.

Cake sighed and rubbed his beard. Was anyone even in here? Maybe they'd all gone off hiking and left their cars and tarps here?

He moved on to the last cabin and knocked on the door. The silence was anticlimactic.

Cake looked around the parking lot with his hands on his hips and sighed.

The sun was firmly up now with barely a cloud in the blue sky. He pulled on a rogue beard hair that seemed to have grown much longer than the others on its own accord.

He turned back to face the door and tried the handle cautiously. The door nudged inwards and his heart leapt.

"I'm coming in! I mean… eh… I'm sorry if I'm disturbing you. I'm naked!" He stopped to wait for a reply, but the cabin was even more quiet on the inside. "Ok, I'm really coming in now and I'm naked but I'm harmless!"

I'm harmless, well that should put everyone at ease. Good job.

"I just don't have any clothes on and I'm sorry about this!"

Oh god, I sound like a fucking loon!

"I'm really nice! I'm just cold and hungry and my brother stole my clothes and he's an asshole and I was wondering if I could maybe get some food or covers and a ride from you to go kick his ass," Cake babbled pushing the door completely open.

The cabin was dark and stuffy with a distinct smell of rotting fruit. A fat fly was angrily bopping against a window at the back of the living space.

All of the cabins in this small bunch had the same layout from the outside and Cake assumed they probably looked pretty much the same on the inside as well: a single large living space with wide windows opposing the front door, facing a few trees and a wild field. The woodwork had been left bare inside which he really appreciated. It let the grain of the wood shine, and gave the dark cabin a cozy feel. He wished he had his camera with him. In the evening the sun would set to the other side of the house and he guessed the light might be fantastic then. Just put a little blueberry pie there on the table next to the back windows and you'd have a full page spread in Martha Stewart Living.

There were two large couches that probably pulled out to beds, with a selection of child-sized clothes and flannel blankets strewn on them. Bedrooms were off to the left, two of them with a bathroom sandwiched between them. A small but functional kitchenette was stuffed at the right hand corner of the room, a few steps from the front door. There were more well fed flies examining the plates on the table in the middle of the room. It looked like a few people might've had pancakes there the night before. The plates were there, the pancakes and people not.

Cake stood in the doorway and listened. Maybe breathing? Were people still sleeping after all the noise he made? He carefully stepped in and made his way to the closed bedroom doors. His hands were sweating and making the foot he was holding slippery.

He held his breath.

No noise.

Was this really a good idea, he considered. He'd just go in and check if there was anyone in.

But I'm naked, a thought popped into his head as he tiptoed further in.

Yes, but I'm also hungry and already inside their cabin, he reasoned with it while pushing down a door handle.

The bedroom was empty. The bed was unmade and mossy air clung to the textiles like a fake beard, but nothing else was there.

These people are not good ventilators, Cake thought chewing on the inside of his cheek. Partly this was from disappointment, but mostly because the failure to air out your room after you've slept in it irritated him.

The next room was in a similar state, only instead of the double bed like in the other room, there was a single bed and Spider-Man slippers next to it. They looked far too big to belong to the child whose clothes were on the living room sofa.

Cake sauntered back to look at the kitchen. The remnants of the pancakes had hardened in the cups and pots. The fridge had an overpowering smell and he debated if it was even worth looking into, but natural curiosity won over common sense and he opened the door only to immediately regret ever walking in through the door.

Everything in the fridge was moldy. Even the tupperware containers were covered in mold, and the mold had different colored mold on top of it. There wasn't a single item in there that would've been anything but liquid with a hefty dose of penicillin. The stench was so much worse now freed from the fridge's confines to wander the empty cabin.

Cake slammed the door shut and could hear things bursting and toppling over inside. Eyes watering he stepped outside to try and catch his breath again.

Whoever had been staying in that cabin hadn't been there in a while and he was now very glad he'd never rented one of these houses as property maintenance at the park seemed to leave a lot to be desired.

A few deep breaths and he dove back in. The stench was slowly making its way across the room and it wasn't showing signs of relenting. Holding his nose, Cake grabbed a fleece blanket from one of the sofas and tried blinking through the tears for anything else he could borrow (there was a faint possibility the people staying in the cabin might have left the park for good, but in case they returned, he didn't feel comfortable taking anything actually valuable). There was a casket of small water bottles in the corner with just a few missing. Cake lunged for them, nabbed one, then dashed back out again, physically trying to duck the prongs of the spreading stench.

The fresh woodland air only hit him after he'd reached the lower steps. The two different airs battled over dominance, the crisp outdoor air at the top, the rotting indoors oozing at the bottom. Cake inhaled deeply. His lungs tingled as the mold and decay were expunged.

Standing there waiting for the mountain breeze to blow away the stench, he closed his eyes and popped open the water bottle.

Water had never tasted so good, nor chilled his entire body so to the very core.

He emptied the entire bottle and let out a relieved sigh, then ducked quickly back in to grab another bottle. Once he had the cabin mapped mentally, the second time was much quicker.

Brushing the remains of the second water bottle from his beard, he could hear quiet rips and tugs; the deer had come back and were determined to make good food of the tarp.

Cake took a menacing step forward: "Boo!"

The deer jumped but didn't run off. They stayed put, ears poised and necks long, staring directly at him.

"Get off that tarp, you idiots!" He waved the fleece towel towards them.

The deer stared silently, their fluffy tails twitching. Then the group parted to make way for

2 large bucks with wide, elaborate antlers perched as crowns.

Cake gulped. Those were very big antlers and the bucks didn't look as impressed with him as he was with them. They could've even looked a little hostile.

"Look, I'm just trying to save you a lotta trouble," he said, lowering his hands palms forward, like he was talking to a herd of unruly bikers.

The bucks took a few steps forward, their hard hooves looking very sharp against the asphalt. They lowered their heads.

"Oh no...."

Cake had little time to think before the herd started charging.

The water bottle went hurtling against the beasts, bouncing of a buck's antlers and spilling into its eyes, momentarily confusing it, but the rest remained on their course, charging ahead in a frightening mass of fluffy white tails and sharp edges. Cake had never run that fast in his life. The pounding of those delicate but deadly hooves behind him as he scrambled back towards the main road and the park entrance and safety, sounded like blades against rock as the herd trampled after him. He pressed faster, the air spikes and blood in his lungs and the asphalt tearing into his bare soles, but these were minor scrapes weighing against his total annihilation. He pounded as fast as his not entirely short human legs could carry him, his prosthesis in one hand, the fleece blanket in the other and his free testicles bouncing erratically from one thigh to the other. Their skin stretched and ached as they swatted around according to momentum, raising tears in his eyes. It didn't matter. It couldn't matter. All that mattered was not getting trampled by a thousand little hammers.

The steady slapping of his bare feet punctuated the painful splats of his private parts and after a while that was all he could hear sprinting ahead. Thud thud thud, splat splat splat, thud thud thud, until his lungs were shriveling up in pain and the blood in his mouth was real. Cake was forced to slow down. He peeked over his shoulder expecting to see the approaching furry death, but they were nowhere to be seen.

He stumbled forward a few more steps, wiping spit from his beard before stopping altogether and slumping to the ground. The deer hadn't followed. Somewhere between the parking lot and where Cake was sitting now they'd decided they'd made their point and stopped following.

Exhausted, he laid down on the road to catch his breath. The sky was still a cheerful blue with a few more white puffs here and there. The sun was as warm as ever. He hadn't died and Cake was grateful for that.

8.

Two hours of walking barefoot turned out more painful than he'd thought. His dash to safety had ripped open the soft skin around his missing toes and now Cake was limping uncomfortably. The things he was seeking revenge on for Brutus were starting to pile up.

The main road widened into the main entryway, a wide space maybe a hundred yards both ways. On the other side he could see the archway of dark pine logs framing the main entrance. To the right, the side he was limping towards, was the park rangers' lodge; a light beige two-story building with three park ranger cars decorated in the park's official green and orange cutout front. On the left side, there was a wide wooden building with a domed roof. It had the gift shop and the restaurant and a bait shop. There was a bus on the other side of the gift shop building, windows dark and the door open.

Cake climbed the steps to the ranger's lodge scanning for Brutus' car parked somewhere along the edge of the woods, but couldn't spot it. There were only a few civilian vehicles there aside from the bus, and he wasn't sure if a tourist bus counted as a civilian vehicle.

The door was open and this time he didn't announce himself.

Cake had tied the blanket around his waist as a makeshift kilt and felt fairly confident that the rangers wouldn't take offense to seeing a semi-naked visitor, who'd at least put an effort in covering himself up. There must've been other similar incidents. Other visitors' whose jerky, about-to-get-his-ass-kicked brothers had played practical jokes and gotten them stranded naked in the middle of wilderness.

A state park might've been organized wilderness, but it was still wilderness, Cake thought grimly. He quickly glanced to the edge of the opening to scan the treeline. No deer.

The rangers' lodge wasn't a large building. It had a dingy nurse's office in the back, stocked with a few basic necessities anyone might need if they were bitten by a snake or fell off a cliff and were bleeding to death but had to hold it in until the medivac chopper got to the scene. There was a tall desk where people picked up their licenses and a small kitchen behind it with cupboards and a coffee machine. A solitary small couch was pushed against the wall opposite the front desk, with an equally small wooden side table. The walls were decorated with plaques, trinkets and a calendar of the park, which presumably the rangers never got tired of looking at. The building was freezing.

"Hello! Anyone here!? I need assistance!" Cake leaned over the front desk to check no one was hiding on the floor. The floor was empty aside from a chair and a pair of sensible boots.

"I've been abandoned and my feet are bleeding!" he tried again.

He was met with only silence and the steady ticking of a wall clock. The clock pointed to 1.30pm.

Cake rounded the reception area and tried the light switch on the wall, but it did nothing. He tried all of them and none of them worked.

The phone was next. He hesitated picking up the bulky office phone with, what seemed to him, an unnecessary amount of buttons and things that might potentially light up, for transferring calls or multiple lines or speakerphones. His magazine had exclusively used cell phones, not physical switchboards, and this monstrosity looked like it was from the early 2000s, or even older than that. Vintage. It was bulky and alien and intimidating.

He picked up the handle. There was no sound. He poked a few random buttons that clicked under his fingers but made no difference in producing a reaction of any kind.

"Come on guys, you gotta have actual cell phones here somewhere, right? Nobody is this ancient...," he mumbled trying to pull open locked drawers under the desk. There were no cell phones there or under the papers spread in uneven piles. Nothing but permit slips and postcards of bears.

"Fine," he spat out, frustrated and moved to the nurse's office to find something for his feet.

As he sat down on the couch to clean and band aid his soles, Cake started taking stock:

His clothes were gone, Brutus was gone or at least parked more than 10 feet outside the front entrance. He hadn't seen a single car driving past when he'd walked over and the electricity was off. *Was there an evacuation?* Wild fires happened. They would sweep through the park area... maybe they'd been evacuated. At night. When he was asleep? They'd been evacuated and his goddamn sonnavabitch asshole of a former brother just fucking took his clothes and drove off? A flash of profound, indignant anger burned Cake's neck and ears. He knew Brutus could be an asshole, but this much? He stopped and stared off into middle distance with a band aid in his hand.

No. No, he probably wasn't that much of an asshole.

There's a difference between feeding your baby brother worms when you're six and abandoning them to be burned alive when nothing looked like there was a catastrophic rush to evacuate.

Or was there? It might not be wildfires. It might be something else. A gas attack? Anger rattled around his head again, making his ears turn red.

He taped the band aid over the chafed scar tissue and pulled the prosthetic on. Looking at it, wiggling his remaining toes through the fake foot seemed somehow odd.

You're overreacting, it's the middle of the day and everyone's out to lunch and the tourists are off on beaches and there just happens to be a power out, he reasoned. *I bet a ranger will walk in any minute now.* He slumped down on the couch, feet aching, feeling safe from wilder beast with sharp hooves, and quickly fell asleep.

Three hours later the hum of rain woke him up. It banged softly against the windows and the metal roof. The sound was homely when listened from indoors, wrapped in a warm fleece blanket. The rain poured down harder as Cake watched unmoving, at the even dark mass of clouds from the bottom of the couch. The wall clock ticked its own, calming tune.

But nothing had changed. If someone had come in while he slept, they hadn't woken him up and that seemed a little unreasonable to Cake. A nice gesture, for sure, but he was still a naked man sleeping in a place where you generally shouldn't see a lot of naked men (he assumed) or people sleeping.

The rain started easing off, and light flickered between the clouds and in through the windows again.

A deep, stabbing pain punched Cake in the gut. Hunger. He hadn't eaten anything all day and now it was almost 5 in the afternoon and his belly was tired of being ignored. He begrudgingly rolled off from the couch and fastened his fleece garment. There had to be something to eat here. Candy bars, trail mix. Anything. He rummaged through the kitchen cabinet, finding mostly coffee cups with inspirational quotes and bags of tea.

The lower drawers had cutlery, and a box of rat poison. The nurse's office wasn't much better, with nothing but a tin of breath mints, which Cake poured into his mouth. Now he felt ill with hunger and mint, but his mouth was also numb. He considered it an uncomfortable compromise.

The gift shop.

The gift shop sold those freeze dried meals and rock candy, he remembered.

The asphalt was still wet under his feet as he dashed over to the other side of the opening, quickly reaching the dome's awning. Rain had pooled into a large puddle next to the building, now reflecting the clear sky with bright oily streaks. Moisture stuck to his skin.

The gift shop's automatic door was half ajar. Between the slit, a streak of leaves, water and dirt stretched on to the otherwise pristine shop floor. The doors put up no resistance as he pushed them to the side. There, there it was right in front of him; row of candy bars, and artisanal, hand-made treats, a selection most Walmarts would be envious of. It was the most beautiful thing he had ever seen.

Cake lunged towards the candy without thinking, then stopped, while already holding a Snickers bar. It wasn't his. None of this was his. His heart was beating fast like a starving man's, holding food within inches of his mouth hole. *This is stealing,* his brain helpfully reminded.

Yes. It is. His hand shook squeezing the chocolate tight.

They have so much though. So much food. His eyes darted from one end of the 35 foot display rack to the other. It was full. Full and pristine, and that didn't even include the hand packaged special candies in baskets near the checkout.

I need it though. And it's not stealing if I pay them back, Cake stared at the candy bar, his heart beat easing off. "It's just borrowing," he mumbled, "did you hear that?! I'm borrowing your candies! Because I'm hungry!"

There was no reply.

"I'm eating it now!" he shouted with a mouth full of Snickers. "And I'm probably gonna eat another! I'm really hungry! I'm sorry!"

The second candy bar was almost as delicious as the first, though he could feel his stomach resisting the sudden rush of sugar and peanuts. But he was determined to power through it.

The candy made him thirsty.

There was a Coca-cola cooler at the other end of the candy rack, the red facade sad and abandoned with the lights off. It had rows of water bottles in it. Cake waltzed over. "Amma take your water too! Sorry!" he exclaimed, before corking a bottle and gulping it down greedily. "Your water is good! Thank you! And I'm sorry!" he shouted up to the dark ceiling. Nothing came back. Not even a whisper or a croak. It seemed even the pigeons had left the park. Cake paused.

"Look, I don't mind if you arrest me for this! You totally should! I'm practically stealing!" he shouted.

It felt wrong to use the word stealing because he was just borrowing for a grave need and would pay them back, but in his heart he knew he was probably technically stealing. But maybe a security camera would catch him, and if nothing else, they'd come and get him. He'd get a ride into the nearest city.

He peered up around the gift shop looking for security cameras, and found only two: one near the front doors and one pointed at the space behind the cash register. Trying for a direct eye contact with whoever was watching behind the cameras, he picked a new candy bar and positioned himself behind the counter. He kept his gaze steady, defiantly staring at the mechanical eye, as he carefully peeled the candy bar open and stuffed it in his mouth, whole. There. His crimes were now definitely on tape. *Come and get me, coppers.*

Cake wandered around the shop. Looking at the bottles in the upright cooler, some had bright colored scum floating near the bottom while the top as filled with lighter liquid. Cake grimaced. Maybe people coming to the park were too health-conscious to buy these things, but he felt the store should consider replacing them every now and then. He grabbed another water bottle, and moved back to where the food was, picking a few more candy bars that looked like things he hadn't tried before. As he stood there looking out through the glass doors, chewing on a protein bar and taking sips of his water, his mind relaxed into listening for cars or distant sirens. Neither seemed to be forthcoming. After a good 20 minutes, he'd finished his lunch and his stomach was protesting. It didn't seem to think this was a proper meal and shad decided to expel it.

Cake needed to go.

Right now.

Frantically rooting around the store for signs, he hobbled deeper in hunched over, as sudden cramps braced his torso and unnatural sounds rang through his stomach linings, rippling through his taut abs. His stomach swell. This was an emergency now. Finally he spotted the customer restroom sign at the very back of the store, and burst in throwing his fleece skirt off just in time, as his bowels exhaled in deep baritone.

It felt like the cacophony of loose expulsions would last forever. It was the single most cathartic experience he'd felt in his life and he certainly was happy it was over, but at what cost. He felt most of the things he'd just put in had come right out.

Cake finished his business and pulled the lever. His makeshift loin cloth lay abandoned a few feet away so he bent to pick it up. Something didn't seem right.

He straightened up tying the fleece around his waist and went back into the booth. There was an odd silence. Nothing to hear. Not a drip or a drop.

Cake carefully lifted the toilet seat up; the bowl was empty. Completely empty. All the water had gone and there was nothing coming in.

Oh great, so the toilets don't work? He frowned at the toilet, lips in a thin line. Fine. The police would be there to pick him up soon anyway. This place was falling apart. He let the seat fall back down with maybe a bit more force than necessary.

By late evening, Cake was sitting in a display canoe flipping a How To guide for bear skinning and hat making. He'd paced around the store for a while but since nothing seemed to be happening, he'd decided to make himself comfortable. In for a penny, in for a pound. He'd arranged a few large flashlights on the shelf behind him like night lights, and put a larger battery operated lantern on the floor next to the canoe. He'd opened some blanket packages and felt fairly cozy under them even if the canoe wasn't the most comfortable place to sleep. It dawned on him that it was probably why they sent dead people down the river in them; the dead didn't need to feel cozy or comfortable, they just needed to move from this world to the next in a blazing fire. And canoeing while alive generally didn't involve sleeping. Or fire.

A large wooden wall clock in the shape of a bald eagle ticket away merrily over the counter. It was well past 9pm and there were still no sirens or flashing lights or any sound of cars. The sun had set in a brilliantly red display, and night had taken over.

He looked up from his book, abandoning the technical details of stitching irregular pelt parts together, and just stared out the window above the front door. Moonlight was trickling in slowly but surely over the display racks, pooling on the floor and rising along the themed t-shirts.

Cake walked to the door. The moon seemed to take up half the sky and the rest was heavy with stars. It was beautiful. A serene silver disc illuminating the trees and ground with borrowed light. This was the best part of camping, he thought. Nights like these. Blue moon and the Milky Way. But as beautiful as this was, he wanted to go home. This joke had gone on far enough and he was ready for a hot shower...

Neither the Moon nor the night sky were giving him any answers, so he pulled the shop doors closed and went back to the canoe, curling up between the books and the flashlights for the night. The police could wake him up in the morning.

9

The morning brought no police.

When Cake woke up, there were still no sirens, no police or military men clearing people out. There were no new cars or old cars. Everything was where he'd left it the night before.

Cake picked a few more trail mix bars from the candy section, then after a moment of deliberation, a small pouch of handmade chocolate truffles, and enjoyed them in his canoe. He picked another stall in the bathroom to do his morning business. The water was still not refilling. After the morning routines he paused to think:

The park seemed abandoned. For whatever reason, Brutus had gone off with his clothes and was going to get a good thumping for it. He needed to get home to find Brutus and beat his ass. This was what he knew for certain.

Cake looked around the shop. Since the police weren't coming to get him, he'd have to walk to the nearest bus stop – which was at least a 2 hour walk – or hitch a ride home. Most people probably wouldn't pick up a naked man in a toga from the side of the road.

He brushed his hand through his hair while thinking and noticed he'd never let his hair down after getting out of the pool. It was still tied up in his usual two small top buns. He'd have angel curls for days. This made him even more grumpy as he started pulling the buns open while wandering around the store looking for fitting clothes he could borrow.

His hair unfurled easily, and the shiny curls cascaded along his back and shoulders. Cake slipped the silver strings he used for tying them up on his wrists and picket a t-shirt off the rack.

Since I'm borrowing stuff, I guess it wouldn't hurt to borrow a jacket too. It might rain again.

He picked up a jacket, some sensible but cheap hiking boots (not the top end five fingered ones in the display case because those were just too expensive. He wasn't inclined on going to prison for an unreasonable 300 percent markup.) and underwear. Pulling them on, while tinged with guilt, felt almost as good as slipping between fresh, crisp sheets. His balls sighed in relief as they nestled naturally in the provided support. Cake did a few test bounces. Things felt packed away. This underwear would work well if he'd have to run away from more deer.

He pulled on the shirt and... it was too small. The waist was perfect but he could barely move his arms and struggled to pull the shirt back up over his head. He checked the label but it was the same size he always wore.

"Are they doing vanity sizing for men's clothes now too? That's just dumb," he grumbled into his beard while looking for a shirt a few sizes bigger.

Sock, pants, extra candy, and water and he was standing outside in the morning light, covering his eyes against the sun. A warm breeze was already starting to dry his locks, now floating along majestically behind him in a way he didn't notice himself.

Something was missing. He could feel a part of a puzzle gone, but couldn't quite place it... a watch! A watch would be useful. He could tell the time when he could be expecting to see a bus. The water resistant wrist watches in glass cases were too expensive and he didn't want to pay for the broken casing. Standing there rubbing his lush beard, he heard the soft ticking of the wall clock.

A few minutes later he'd wiggled it down and made a hasty chain for it from shoelaces, to hang it around his neck. He felt vaguely irreverent to society's norms, which cheered him up.

Cake started off through the main entrance.

An hour of walking towards Iona and he hadn't yet run into a bus, a passing car, or the police. He'd seen a single empty car crashed into a tree about a mile away from the entrance. Those were fairly common in areas with wild animals and forest so near the road. People would swerve for squirrels and deer and end up off the road their cars totalled. It might take a day or two for anyone to come tow the wrecks away. This one didn't seem burned, just squished like a bean around the tree. There was no saving it, the owner would need to get a brand new car. If there still was an owner.

Cake shook his head to flush out the morbidity. All that car was good for was reminding others it was a bad idea to swerve squirrels. He'd walked past without giving it much more thought, long hair flowing in the gentle breeze.

The sun was high and on his skin. The walking didn't seem bad at all, even if he was getting a little hungry again, so he pulled one of the raw food bars from his pocket and munched on it traipsing down the road. The trees were starting to depart from the roadside, edged out by the approaching fields. Cake swore he had walked almost half way to his mom's by now, without a single car passing by. Of course, he wasn't even a third of the way there, but it sure felt like it when walking. His thighs tingled.

The road curved slightly to the right and the last remaining trees revealed a service station just ahead, nestled in the middle of potato fields pushing up greens. The saplings were still low, but persistent. Cake picked up his pace. Since he hadn't seen bus stops, or buses, the station was his next best bet in finding someone to give him a lift. The familiar friendly skunk in the neon sign smiled mischievously at him, and Cake felt his body relaxing.

One of the pumps was occupied. The nozzle was firmly stuck in the car's tank, but no one seemed to be looking after it. There were two other cars parked to the side and a pickup at the back. The front wall was covered by a litter of bicycles. The lights were off on the inside.

As silent as the station was, no radio sounding off from the inside and no one shouting about leaving the pump nuzzle in the car while paying for your gas, Cake felt optimistic. A little ways off from the station, maybe a half a mile away along the road, there were other buildings, homes and tackle shops, in a small cluster. People lived here. They had decent food, phones, computers and mortgages. He'd stopped by this station a few times before, and eaten at the Shrimp And Hot Dog restaurant hidden in the middle of that cluster. Cake stared into the horizon trying to see movement between the buildings, but his eye sight wasn't good enough. He reached for the station door.

A sweet draft escaped through the door.

Cake stepped in and the smell hit him hard. It was like the fridge at the park lodge, if the fridge was the entire building. Everything but cans had spoiled. Anything in bags, everything in the standing coolers, all of the jugs of milk... oh god, all of the milk!

He felt bile rise up in his throat and lunged out the door retching. The sunny outdoors only offered marginal relief. The smell was still there, clinging to his newly stolen clothes and writhing through his hair, and no amount of glass doors was going to fully contain it.

There was clearly a problem with the electricity. There seemed to be a problem with people not being there to fix the electricity as well.

Cake caught his breath leaning on his knees. He stared at the ground intently. What was going on? No one would leave their service station in that condition, would they? And where were the customers whose cars were parked there?

"Where is everyone!?" he yelled first cautiously, then more confidently. "Hellooo!!!? Come on! This is fucking stupid and weird! Stop it!". His voice carried over the fields and rustled up a flock of birds. That was all the movement he managed to stir up. Nothing else came back from the fields or the store.

Cake cupped his mouth with his hands; "I'm tired of this! I gotta long way to go home! I need a lift! And you guys are being assholes! It's not fucking funny!"

The wind pushed potato saplings around and stirred the grass on the side of the road. Then it died down.

Really? Desperation flushed over him and his shoulders sank as he thought how far away home still was. He could be walking for days.

Days.

The sun glinted off the row of small bicycles as he crouched. He stared at them for a moment. *Goddamn.*

This bicycle was not meant for someone over 6 foot tall. It was meant for someone who was at the most 4 and a half feet, and liked things that made a lot of noise the faster you pedaled.

The little noisemakers in the spokes had been the first to go.

He'd picked the bike that seemed the tallest, but that was chained firmly to a flower pot, so he'd had to settle for the smaller, unlocked, bike with every bell and whistle a teen could ever want. After a mile, he had to stop to violently beat the noise making accessories off the wheels.

He'd ventured inside the service station to get some non-perishable foods, which still seemed to smell. The stench of rot was now permanently etched into everything in there. Then he'd gotten some paper and written a note to the teen whose ride he'd borrowed. He stashed the note under a rock next to the other bicycles, in case anyone came back wondering why their bicycle was missing. He could maybe work off a bicycle debt in a year or two. He wasn't paying for the noisemakers, though. That debt had already been settled.

The bike was decidedly not his size, but Cake still felt this was possibly the best theft so far, aside from the food and underwear. The distance was passing by at twice the speed, even if it was still going to take him hours to get to the outskirts of Iona. But he was enjoying freewheeling down hills.

The makeshift town next to the service station had been equally abandoned. Nothing seemed to be moving inside the houses or the stores. The grocery store and the restaurant put off such powerful smells, he hadn't even tried stopping there. He did stop at a crossroads before leaving the town, to pet a cat crossing the street. It was a fat orange and white tabby. No collar or a tattoo. Independent cats were even more common than crashed cars on the sides of the roads here. Farmers liked having them around to protect seed crops from vermin and the cats liked being around lots of food and scritches. The cat had leaned in, blinking lazily as Cake pet it, before suddenly bolting off after an invisible mouse, leaving him alone with his tiny bicycle.

Checking his clock, it was closer to 7pm before Cake saw familiar buildings off in the distance: the edging rows of the suburban sprawl before suburbia transformed into just potato wilderness and endless commercial fields. It gave him the extra boost the raw food bars and ice tea couldn't, to pedal as fast as he could the final miles. The road sloped easily into familiar bends and dead ends and Cake felt his mind relax. He'd sleep between clean sheets tonight. Kick Brutus's ass tomorrow. He'd have a hot shower! He was now freewheeling the corners as the weight of the travel blew away with the breeze.

The houses stood in familiar rows, with cars out front and grass... the grass was very long. Not just on one yard but on every yard. There was an unnatural silence hanging over everything. The evenings were supposed to be the busiest with people coming home from work, pushing kids in and out of cars to get to their hobbies, neighbors greeting each other with distant nods, sprinklers turning on for the evening. But now there was just tall grass covering the sprinklers and pathways.

He slowed down, letting the bicycle roll on its own weight as he eyed the houses, trying to see a flash of a recognizable face. A squirrel running across the road startled Cake and he gripped the handlebar tighter coming to a stop at the curb.

"Hellooo!" he shouted carefully. "Hey!"

The words echoed between the buildings.

The sun had nearly set and none of the streetlights had yet come on even a little bit. A tiny chill made this muscles twitch.

Cake walked his bicycle around the bend to their street. No lights on in the houses. Grass and knotweed had overtaken the yards. Cars stood motionless in the creeping darkness, like beached manatees harboring secrets.

He stopped in front of their house.

The lights were out.

Carefully he pushed open the gate to the yard. No chain or paws came forward. The entire dog house was gone.

"Bob? Bob!!", Cake called out. The grass stayed still. He let the bike fall to the ground as he strode to the front door. The spare key was where it always was. That was something.

The hallway inside was dark. Cake reached for a light switch, but flipping it did nothing. The darkness remained. He pulled out a spare flashlight from the drawer in the hallway but even the drawer felt wrong.

The chair. The fourth chair wasn't there.

In the stingy light the pocket flashlight allowed, he looked around.

"Mom?" Cake called. "Mom, are you home?"

Nothing moved in the dark. Only the same sweet smell emanated faintly from the kitchen. He had a sinking feeling what he'd find there, but unfortunately the kitchen was the only place where his mom kept candles and other emergency supplies, so he ducked into the moist stench deciding to avoid even looking at the fridge. The fridge was a trap. He knew this. But he pushed the thought in the bottom-most corner of his mind because if the fridge was a trap...

Candles of all sizes were in a box under the kitchen island. Matches in the top drawer. Cake rummaged around and found a large industrial-sized torch from the broom closet and now he could almost see in the dim of the house. It looked the same, except darker than during the day. For the most part. The more he looked, the more wrong things became. Like the hallway chair, the round kitchen table was gone. There was small white one with two chairs in its place, leaving a wide, unnatural gap between the table and the nearest counter. The living room also had... fissures. Ruptures in the plan where perfectly fitting items were not fitting perfectly anymore. His mom's priced set of armchairs and a matching ottoman were gone. In their place was a bulky velvet recliner. The couch looked the same to Cake, but there was something off with it. Was it in a different place?

Cake stepped quietly. He didn't even know why he did that, sneaked around like a thief in his mother's house.

"Mom? Bob? Are you upstairs? Are you decent, mom?". Maybe she was sleeping or naked or had a 'special guest', though she'd only had one of those since the divorce, but it could happen. Adults did that. Cake glared at the intrusive thought, his ears listening to the darkness.

No one answered back. Hesitantly, he started on the stairs, the torch painting a weird bottom-of-the-bottle shape on the walls where the spotlight hit them. He could hear his own breathing as his free hand reached for the wall for support, only to land on a new rail on the side none had been before. A stair lift track ran across the wall, easily masquerading as skirting. The seat was parked at the top of the stairs, opposite to the bedroom door. His fingers glided over the cool metal rail.

The stairs and upper floor were pitch black. The torch only made a dim beige halo in the darkness and his footsteps were swallowed by the carpeting. The rush of blood in his veins made more sound than the world around him.

Cake stopped in front of his mother's bedroom.

"Mom? Mom, are you there? Mom, I'm coming to your room. Please be decent," Cake stated to the door, his hand uneasy on the handle.

The door blocked his voice.

It didn't answer back.

Neither did anyone in the room behind it. *Mom is sleeping*, Cake kept repeating. Everything was ok. It was late. Everyone was tired. It was all going to be alright. Mom would laugh. Stupid dark houses making his stupid lizard brain freak out. "Ok, I'm really coming in now because this is all getting really creepy and I want you guys to stop it already," he whispered pushing the door open.

"Mom?"

10.

There was a lump on the bed.

The bedroom was the largest in the house. Janet had treated herself when she finally could afford it after the divorce and gotten a king-size bed, which ate into the bedroom space, but not too much to make it claustrophobic.

That bed was gone. There was a bed, but it wasn't... right. It was smaller. It was smaller and one end was propped up like a hospital bed's.

It was a hospital bed. The beige wheels poked out from under a curtain of bedding hanging over the side of the mattress.

"Mom, is that you?" Cake whispered to the dark.

The lump didn't move. He pushed the door open all the way and followed the torch's light as it cut through the dim air hanging from the ceiling and walls. The window was mostly covered, with a flicker of the sky seeping through, but the rest of the room was just shapes, hard to identify as anything. A few steps in from the door, the carpet softly sucking in all sound, and he was standing next to the bed. The lump stayed still.

"Mom?" Cake swallowed.

The shadows on the walls shifted. Wind had picked up and rustled the trees outside.

121

He looked back down on the bed, his heart stuck in his throat.

"Mom?"

Cake reached for the lump to wake her up. *Wake up mom, is everything ok?*

His hand landed on soft folds and through to the mattress as the lump deflated under his touch.

It was just a pile of blankets in a human form, nothing human between them and the sheets.

His mom wasn't there.

Cake's heart skipped and he let out a breath. He didn't know what he'd been expecting but somehow an absence was better than finding something right now.

He flashed the torch around the room steadying himself. What was going on here? When illuminated, the shapes that didn't look like anything started to make sense: There was a drip holder next to the bed and an electric lift. For what? So much machinery, things that didn't belong here at all. The en suite door stood open and vacant. Who slept here? This wasn't his mom's. She didn't need all this.

Cake glanced around the room to find something, anything. The side table was the one he'd helped carry upstairs. The lamp on it was familiar, as was the picture frame under it with the boys as boys, some twenty years ago. Brutus had a toothy grin he'd grow out of. Little Cake looked worried under his blond pudding bowl cut that didn't quite reach his ears. That picture had always been there. The cane leaning to the table was new. It wasn't hers. Cake reached out to pull open the drawers of a nightstand. They were full of bright orange pill bottles. None of these should've been there. She only took medication for her hay fever. But all the bottles were labeled with her name. Xeloda, Tramadol, empty vials of Eloxatin and Camptosar, medicinal lotions and cream tubes. Mostly empty or half empty.

Cake slumped on the bed holding bottles in his hands.

"What happened, mom? How did you ever hide this from me?" he mumbled rolling the vials in his palms. "How long's this been going on?". He turned bottles over to see the dates, as if those would tell him when it all began and...

Filled 5/28/2023

2023

That's a funny error, he thought spreading all of the bottles and ointments on the blanket. All of them had the same year. 2023.

Cake pushed himself off the bed backing up like the bottles were a slow acting poison. "They should've fixed that time stamp at the drug store, eh..." Cold sweat pushed through his skin.

Cake turned on his heel and ducked out the door. He marched through the hallway to his room; the boxes were gone. His bed had neat beige linen he'd never seen, and a small side table with a picture frame on it that didn't belong to him. There was a smiling black woman in it holding a small child. Who were these people? The walls were strangely bare. His posters were gone.

So were the school flags from football games, his certificates, the patch of wallpaper he peeled off from the corner when he took down his Hetalia poster. Painted over. His hand slid down the unnaturally smooth door frame.

He felt ill. Everything strange was catching up to him. It was tentacles in the dark reaching for his edges. It was moonlight pouring in through the window like a slow wave. His heart was beating uncomfortably hard against his ribs.

Cake swung the torch around like something was waiting for him in the dark. Shadows shifted before the beam of light and stayed still around it. Nothing was moving, but he couldn't shake the feeling that everything was, just outside the light. Just behind all the closed doors. Right around the corner. Behind him. Something must've been moving.

He stepped more carefully to Brutus' room and pushed the door open.

It was the same as ever. Brutus' posters were on the walls, his school flags, his collectibles. The walk-in closet in the hall was also the same. Clothes. Towels. Shoes. Nothing moved. All familiar items. All things he'd used. Except for his own things.

Cake stumbled downstairs into the kitchen and started rummaging through the drawers. Bills. Calendars. Planners. Anything. Everything. Anything with number, dates, news. Pens, screwdrivers, screws spilled form the drawers. Post-its stumbled to the floor as his hands fumbled through the murky cabinets identifying shapes with touch then discarding them and moving to the next lump. A box of matches. So many tacks when his mom didn't even have a tack board (or did she? She didn't have yesterday when he left). Rubber bands. Next drawer. Spoons. Sharp edges. His fingers were bleeding.

Next drawer. Paper.

Envelopes.

He pulled out a stack of bills, the bottom ones opened, the top ones still sealed.

Cake shifted the piles into a rainbow over the counter top, attentively examining them under the torch light. His fingers stung as the papers glided under the stabbed skin. The envelopes switched places; electricity there, phone there, miscellaneous in another pile, anything with the Cedar Hill logo or even vaguely medical sounding sender in their own.

Four stacks.

Cake was hunched over, his stomach taut and painful, expecting something to lurch out from reality at any moment as he eyed the piles, the torch spotlight illuminating not really any of them.

So many envelopes in the medical stack… he set his hand on it lightly, paused for a moment, then turned to the others. The opened ones had "paid" scribbled on top in his mother's neat handwriting that dented the cellulose into peaks and valleys in the torch light.

He pulled out the first paid bill: sent January 4th 2023

Discarding it, he moved on to the next: January 17th 2023

The next: February 2023

Next: 2023

2023

2023

2023

2023

20...

The bills slipped from his hands and Cake tumbled to the floor. He couldn't feel his legs. Everything from his shoulders down was cold and numb. The numbness was spreading. His hands hung listless on the floor as he leaned his forehead against a cabinet door. Eyes shut, breathing was so hard. Was there any oxygen in the room? It all seemed so dim. His face was tingling towards his lips... and then everything went dark.

11.

The sun woke up the flies.

There was a space between the kitchen island and the floor. A sliver of a space with a lonely tuft of dust stuck in it.

Cake blinked. The left side of his face felt cold against the floor tiles. Somehow that semi-opaque hair ball was the most normal thing he'd seen in days and he kept staring at it lying on his side and trying to figure out what he should do. He might try getting off the floor. It seemed liked a reasonable idea. Safe enough. Something people did every day.

Pushing himself up, his hands felt uneasy. They slipped along the tiles as the paper bills under them ran off without friction. He propped himself up back against a cabinet door and gathered the bills in his lap.

The first rays of the sun were peeking in through the curtains leaving golden streaks along the walls. His torch lay on the floor slowly dying, as fat flies softly bumbled against the kitchen window above him.

"I don't… I don't understand," Cake muttered, rubbing his beard then continuing the motion and rubbing his entire face in his palm. He pinched his eyes closed. There was a dull ache on his left temple, but it didn't seem to be swollen as he ran his hand over it.

Something was not right, he decided. Something was, in fact, very wrong. And not just in how he'd somehow lost 6 years, or how every company his mother had business with had the same computer glitch in their software's dates. Something was wrong with him.

Cake preened his hair absentmindedly staring at the edges of the cabinets in front of him and the slowly shifting hues of morning light. His hand stopped mid-pull.

"I don't have long hair," he said to the strand of long hair he'd pulled in front of his face that was very much attached to his head from the other end. "And I don't have prosthetics," he said to his left foot wiggling the two fleshy toes poking through a prosthesis that filled in the missing three.

Instinctively he grabbed his leg with one hand and his stomach with the other, *Is this mine?!*

He could feel his hand on his leg and the abdominal muscles moving under the shirt fabric and felt a little relieved. Then alarmed. If he was in his own body and this wasn't a virtual reality simulation or a hallucination, then it probably was 2023 and he'd lost 6 years somehow and that didn't seem like a good thing. He had strong feelings about it.

Cake headed to the upstairs bathroom pulling at his hair deep in thought.

The large window was facing east bathing the entire room in golden light. Looking at his reflection, Cake felt his heart sink. That was him. Him but older. His face was more angular now the puppy-fat had melted away from his cheeks. His beard was thick and his hair thicker, landing in gentle curls over his shoulders and pulling his face into an even more square expression.

He laid the wall clock from his neck on a clothes hamper, and pulled his shirt off. His body was now round and lean with muscles popping out everywhere in places he'd never knew could be muscular. Cake pushed the skin on his stomach around with his finger; there was barely any fat between it and the quiet mounds of muscle under it. When he flexed, it looked like someone pinched his skin back behind him as the muscles strained and veins popped to surface along his arms and biceps. There was a downy fuzz of blond chest hair covering his upper body and small, light scars everywhere. He made some experimental poses in front of the mirror, eyes examining his new dimensions. He frowned at his reflection.

"I ain't mad," he said quietly. "Ok, I'm probably mad, but not at this," he added glaring at himself.

As Cake turned to put his shirt back on, a larger scar on his right arm caught his eye. It wasn't like the small nicks and scrapes riddling his body. This was large and puckered and angry like the new tissue he'd seen on burn victims. It looked like a symbol; four concentric circles leaving a little star shape between them and smaller welts around it emphasizing the star. He traced the protruding edges with his thumb trying to gauge some meaning from it, but nothing surfaced. It was definitely a deliberate shape, at least more deliberate than the random small scars. *Probably didn't get that in a hospital. Not a good hospital anyway.*

"Was I in a gang or something?" he whispered.

The scars didn't answer.

The flies were happily buzzing around a fruit bowl with a mess of half liquefied, half mummified fruit for them to feast. They were busy making more flies. The soft buzzing was an oddly comforting sign of life.

Cake's stomach growled as he stacked the fallen envelopes back on the kitchen counter and tried to turn the torch on and off. It didn't blink. The batteries were done.

As he rummaged around the drawers and cupboards for new batteries, he tried to organize the mess inside his head. What he'd seen last, where he'd seen what last and what was the last thing he should be looking for first.

Mother and Brutus.

Two thick batteries rolled into his palm and he grabbed them a with a grin. "Ha! Gotcha." He unloaded the dead batteries. Working light now. Family. Car. Yes, it would all come together.

The morning mist was slowly condensing on the asphalt leaving it looking slick and new. The tall grass swooned under the weight of droplets and the air was more crisp than anything he'd taken in at national parks in his whole life.

Cake stood on the porch with his arms akimbo squinting at the silent neighborhood. Then he strode to the stocky brown house on the other side of the road.

The buzzer still worked and let out an off-key jingle that disappeared into a whine. He tried again and the bell produced a few more tone deaf tunes.

Nothing moved behind the yellow glass pane next to the door.

Cake knocked on the door, first courteously, then with increasing force, calling out Mr and Mrs Friday. The door shuddered under his fist, but remained still and the house silent.

He made a jaunt around the house, but came up mostly empty: the back yard had a pitcher and two empty glasses on a patio table. Something had dried in all of them a while ago. A dirty blue fleece blanket hung over the side of a lawn chair.

He peered in through the patio doors but the inside of the house was dark. Cake made his way back to the front.

He stomped to the next house and did the same. They didn't have a door bell, so he pounded the door knocker until his ears were ringing. No one was home.

After a few more homes, he stopped on the curb, staring down the street. His stomach was making watery gurgles and his eyes stung, but the rest of the street was indifferent. Morning mist had evaporated with the sunrise and the sun was now merrily pushing clouds away from the morning sky. Leaves waved at each other with the wind and the grass stretched out in waves whenever a breeze ruffled through it. Birds were chirping freely, to welcome the Sun.

This might be part of an evacuation area? Cake reasoned to himself. *If they evacuated the park, maybe they evacuated a larger area? A whole state?* He pulled on his beard.

"Right, hospital. Hospitals would know? They'd have records of where their patients were moved," Cake huffed into his fist.

He stomped back home and through to the garage; Janet's car was there, but his car wasn't. Cake frowned, then headed back into the hallway; he'd seen her handbag on the drawer and proceeded to riffle through it for keys. There was a phone, a strangely light and slim phone, he pulled aside. He poked at the buttons on the sides and shook it, but the charge was gone and now there was nothing he could do to recharge it.

Finding the keys, Cake marched back into the garage. He slammed the garage door button but nothing happened. The door stayed still.

"Oh. Right."

He pulled the door up by hand and got in the driver's seat a little less determined. The car needed a little coaxing, but after a few dry whirs, the engine picked up and Cake leaned back into the driver's seat. The smell of gas was a sliver of comfortable humdrum.

The car was safe. It was normal. Driving a car would be what people did every day and he should do that. He could drive it like he always drove cars.

As he backed out, he could've sworn something glimmered in the corner of his eye, but it was probably just the Sun hitting the side mirror.

12.

The farm land quickly sprouted low brick buildings as he approached the Cedar Hill hospital. The roadsides were populated by vast parking lots for everything and the buildings rested on the other side of the lots in flat clumps. Only a few residential buildings had inched closer to the road, leaving their parking spaces hidden behind them. Cedar Hill was the only building taller than four stories within a five mile radius. More than five. It might've been the only building taller than three stories in the entire town. It also had the most glass. For an emergency care unit, it looked almost fashionable. When Cake was rushed to the ER the first time in early 2000, he'd reasoned that friendly was the emotion the architect had gone for. In reality though, the architect had mostly wanted to disguise the structure so it wouldn't stand out between the businesses and the residentials. After building had finished, he'd been surprised himself how calm and very nearly beautiful the hospital had turned out. "You'd never guess people were losing limbs and bleeding out on the inside" he'd told the contractor, standing out on the parking lot as the trucks and loaders packed up the construction debris. The contractor

134

nodded, not knowing what to say. So he just smiled and signed paperwork trying to avoid eye contact with the architect. The two never worked together on a building again, despite living two blocks from each other.

The parking lot in front of the hospital was one third full, dotted with cars as empty as the ones dotting the road and its sides. Dry grass had collected against their tires and rain dimmed the windshields. Pigeons perched on the roofs defiantly, staring down each other and smaller birds looking to land near by.

Cake rolled slowly through the parking lot once, made a turn at the end, then parked near the emergency entrance. There was an ambulance there, the back door hanging open.

He got out and leaned on the car roof for a moment, breathing in deeply. There wasn't exactly a sweet smell, but then again, hospitals never smelled like other places. Not even their parking lots. It smelled distantly sweet, but mostly it just smelled like rain and dust that hadn't left the asphalt. Not even a lingering scent of fast food. Just... air and heat. The tall, red, brick and glass building stood silently, sunlight reflecting on the myriad windows in a way that he would've found calming under other circumstances.

After a moment of simply admiring the building, Cake finally closed the door and locked the car before hiking to the side of the ambulance. A transparent tube hung from the open door and let out a faint whistling sound when a breeze blew past it. Cake peeked in. Just an open box of medical supplies spilled on the floor, nothing more. The empty gurney was half way through the sliding doors and had jammed between them.

He easily pushed the dead doors open and the gurney in out of the way.

A gust of air blew in to rustle the magazines and papers stacked in the reception.

"Hello! Anyone in!? I got an emergency!" Cake tried.

A wall clock ticked back from the silence.

"I... uh... I got left here when y'all evacuated!" He glanced around looking for security cameras and then waived when he spotted them hanging in the corners of the room. The cameras stared back with their empty glass eyes.

"Ok, fine," Cake whispered under his breath, and ventured behind the reception desk.

The desk was a mess of papers and pens, and the floor didn't look much better. There was bird feces on the counter and two silent pigeons huddled together under a chair. They moved back in unison as Cake approached, but didn't leave, instead ruffled together, then melted into a warm dumpling of comfortable bird-sleep. The papers on the desk had curled and bubbled with moisture, the corners forming into stiff peaks. The computer screens were dead as was a single camera monitor next to them.

I guess no one is watching from these...

Cake pursed his lips together running his hand along the screen. Everything was covered in light dust.

He scanned the desk for clues. A note saying "WE ALL RAN OFF, MEET US AT DENNY'S!" would've been the best, but even just a newspaper headline with a natural disaster would've helped. There was nothing remarkable. Nothing but receipts and damaged papers with names, numbers and dates. No natural disasters. No instructions to the nearest Denny's. No letter with To Whom It May Concern in suspiciously alarmed handwriting. Just regular old work papers. The dates were the same as the ones he'd found at home: 2023. Cake pulled on his beard in frustration as his finger slid along the ink ridges.

Focus, dummy.

He turned to look for a filing cabinet. A large one behind him was locked but the keys were dangling in the lock, and he was soon flipping through the folders inside.

These were not patient files. Administrative files. Receipts. No patient names. He pushed the drawers shut a little more frustrated than he'd been before, and stepped back to stand in the darkened corridor.

The reception was in the middle of the hall, like a watershed island, dividing the traffic to left and right. Going to the right, you'd find a narrower hallway, punctuated by doors to doctors' offices and beyond that, smaller operating rooms. To the left of the reception, exactly opposite to the front door, you'd come to a wide hallway that fed directly to the larger operating room. Cake had been here before, many times. If he wasn't getting stitched up or showing unusual rashes to a concerned doctor, he'd be visiting grandma. She'd spend so many weeks in there, it almost became a tradition. A Johnson family holiday.

Grandma was admitted for 2 days, 5 days, then later weeks and months, after whatever complications she'd had. They'd bring her books and anise bears. She loved the books and claimed to love the bears, but never seemed to eat much of them. She told Cake and Brutus to help themselves, like the candy was a ruse to lure them to the visit. The boys both hated anise bears. Everyone did. Grandma probably hated them too.

With each stay, she got smaller. At home, grandma was soft and round, with white and gold hair in sort curls floating around her head. She smelled like nylon and spices. At the hospital she dried up, became brittle on the outside and the warm smell of spices gave away to the sharp smell of hand sanitizer. Then even that was gone.

Cake stared down at the quiet corridor. Was grandma's the third or the fourth door from the end?

The corridors hadn't changed since he was a kid and it would've been strange if they had since buildings generally stayed fairly static. With the electricity gone, the only light came through windows and leaked weakly into the hallways from under doors. Cake flicked his torch on, swinging it from door plaque to door plaque. Surely they'd have an office or a main archive or something with actual patient files. It couldn't all be on the computer.

He randomly pushed open doors with no indicators on them, only to find room dividers and metal stools and small carts with medical equipment in them. Or tables and cardboard boxes that were clearly meant to be in a different part of the hospital with their contents neatly packed to shelves. Further down, past glass doors, you'd enter the inpatient ward, with nothing but rooms filled with empty beds, the sheets disheveled and jackets and purses hung on hooks on walls. People had been here. They'd been staying here, but somehow left without enough time to grab their coats, purses, or shoes. Cake was starting to have doubts about his evacuation theory, but pushed it out of his mind. Where else could they have gone? It's not like there were bloody marks on the floor, of people being dragged through air vents, or broken windows from riots. No, everything was neat. Neat-ish. As neat as you could leave something in the middle of the day if you just had to pop out for groceries, while you were being wheeled in to the emergency room.

The though of groceries made his stomach lurch uncomfortably again. Stomach acid pushed up his throat. He gulped hard to push it back down and rubbed his eyes. He needed food, but he needed to find mom first.

In one of the patient rooms, reddish brown ankle boots were neatly stuffed under a bed. Cake wandered in, attracted by the color. The room was light with big windows providing all the exposure anyone could ever need and a lovely view over the surrounding malls, stores and parking lots. Off in the distance, beyond the parking lots, the silent highway drew a line between civilization and the wilderness.

He saw no cars on it.

He picked up one of the shoes and turned it over in his hand. A sock dropped out of it and he quickly set the shoe back where he'd found it. A woman's green pea coat hung on the wall, dark green buttons punctuating the front, and a reddish brown scarf on top unfurled in lurid contrast. Cake shook his head and moved the bed linens to the end of the bed. There was nothing remarkable there. Just an empty bed and another on the opposite side of the room. He noticed his reflection in the window, hair still hovering in a wild mane around his shoulders, and set the torch on the bed. He quickly pulled his hair into two sections, the rolled them up and twisted them into two small flat buns on top of his head, securing both with the silver strings around his wrists. It was an automatic movement. He didn't need to think about it before the hair was secured and he only stopped to thinking why he'd done that, where he'd gotten the strings, after he was back in the corridor. His free hand instinctively flew up to touch one of the buns.

It felt just like it should. It made him more confident; a feeling that slightly scared him. He made a mental note to figure out how he knew how to do his hair like that.

Coming back from the patient side he passed by elevator doors and next to them, a stairway with a sign indicating cold storage and archives.
Finally!
The door was open and Cake bounced down the stairs to basement level landing in another corridor, but this time with even less light.
COLD STORAGE said the sign to the left.
"Why do they need cold storage-... oh. Ooooh..."
Cake eyed nervously down the pitch black hallway to the left. There wouldn't be ice cream down that route. He chewed on his cheek and followed the signs to the right determined not to care about the storage on the left. And not to look behind his back. The door to archives wasn't very far away and by luck, it too would be unlocked. Nope, there wasn't a left turn down here. There was definitely nothing behind his back. There was no such thing as cold storage.

The archives were unlocked.
Stepping into the room, Cake realized the archives room wasn't a room. It was a hall. It was several halls encased in concrete walls reaching down further than the torch light would ever carry, each hall at least 30 feet by 30 feet. The walls

were covered in metal storage shelves stacked without breaks with paper folders. Each folder was bursting with papers. Along the center of the halls, identical shelves with identical folders ran down into the darkness. It all reminded him of something. A library? No, something bigger. He looked down the infinite shelving. Shelves reaching higher than the ceiling. Geometrical windows doming over him somewhere so far up the light barely reached the bottom floors. Tall figures gliding silently between columns, lights in their hands, trailed by cumbersome metal that waddled noisily as it imitated walking. The thuds and whispers echoed in his mind.

There was no one there in this archives room.

Cake's eyes returned to the folders.

He stepped closer and ran his fingers down the closest row. There were easily a hundred slips of paper in a single folder. Cake sighed. This could take him a while.

He started pulling folders out, checking the edges of the shelves, turning papers around trying to figure out the filing system, thumbing idly at the colorful tapes at the edges. Pretty primary colors in glossy tape. Block letters next to them. It made the folders look cheery, he thought.

Decorated folders.

His hand stopped as he squinted.
The glossy tape wasn't there to cheer the staff up. It wasn't like in the movies: there weren't drawers filled with folders, with headlines like "important evidence", "Plot McGuffin"...

No, the colorful tapes **were** the system. The non-alphabetical block letters **were** the system.

And he had no idea how to decode any of it.

He panned around the archive shelves with the torch, a crushing feeling tightening his chest. Thousands. Thousand upon thousands of records, folders, notes. All under bright cheery tape and inaccessible letter combinations. All folders stuffed with hundreds if not thousands of sheets of paper with different patient names. How many Janet Johnsons would there be? How many different records of his mother in here? She could be in a thousand different places, on a thousand different dates, slipped between thousands of other patients.

He couldn't breathe.

Cake gasped for air as his cheeks turned red. An invisible fist was squeezing his heart. He couldn't find her here. Not before he'd grow old and die down in some concrete bunker under an abandoned hospital, next door to all the other dead people they kept here.

He glanced at the darkened corridor outside the archive door. Maybe he should just stay here. Stay and stop. Forget everything.

He screwed his eyes shut tightly. No, what sort of quitter talk was this. *You need to eat, you're talking crazy.*

He let out the breath he'd been holding and opened his eyes.

The folder in his hands was useless. He could find out about all sorts of weird boils or stitches people he'd never met had gotten, but these wouldn't tell him about his family. And they wouldn't tell him where they were.

He returned the folder to where he'd pulled it and walked back upstairs, a little more somber.

Just as he'd remembered, there was still a canteen at the other side of the hospital. It felt smaller than before, but had more vending machines lining the sides of the entrance. Cake frowned at the blue and green coke bottles shining like neon lights from the soda machine. "Blue raspberry coke? Maybe this really is the future," he muttered heading towards the check out.

The check out till was decorated with baskets, jars, and boxes of small snacks. Cake hovered over them feeling his mouth water and stomach churn like a broken hard drive. He was far past being just hungry. The nausea and lightheadedness of low blood sugar wallowed behind his eyes as he loomed over the snack bars. One wouldn't hurt, would it?

He quickly grabbed a small protein bar and stuffed it in his pocket, glancing around nervously. Then he straightened up and grabbed a small water bottle hiding it behind his back.

His eyes darted from side to side around the canteen expecting someone to object from behind a table or from a back room. No one objected.

He made two long strides towards the cafeteria entrance covering the water bottle with his free hand, and pushed the door open with his backside. The exit opened up to another parking lot on the other side of the building. He stopped to pan around the cafeteria one more time, then dashed outside into the bright noon light.

Sitting outside on a bench next to the doors, he slowly chewed on his ill-gained snacks and sipped on the water. Where now? He could drive to New Port and ask his friends what'd happened to Idaho, though if he'd been gone for 6 years, there was no way of knowing if any of them still lived in the same places. Brutus lived in the other direction. He'd been a Nevada resident for a few years, but had a habit of moving around after projects every year or two and Cake had never visited him in his last address in Boulder City.

Finishing the protein bar, he realized he didn't even have that address on him. It was on his phone, but his phone... he had no idea where that was either.

And dad...

Cake's mouth pressed into a thin white line.

Talina! She if anyone would still be in the same place, she'd be it.

Cake watched as the wind jostled an empty styrofoam cup along the parking lot. A further off a plastic bag had taken flight.

He leaned his head in his hands. There was a weird pressure-like sensation in his ears. It wasn't quite like pressure, but almost like having water stuck in them. When you couldn't hear properly. When everything sounded muted. But worse. Now the sound was all the way off.

Cake coughed and his own voice startled him. The echo quickly faded off into the vastness of the parking lot. It wasn't that the sounds were muted. It was that there were no sounds. It was the absence of The Hum. The Hum that had underscored every day of his life before this. The distant sound of traffic on highways.

It was gone.

Now it was just the birds and the wind and him, making noises into the universe.

Cake looked over the parking lot and for the first time, the lack of other people felt vast and permanent.

13.

There was a dead pigeon lying right next to the front doors of Target. On aisle 2 Cake found a dead chickadee. He picked both birds up wearing garden gloves and found an empty shoe box to put them in. The box he left on the customer service desk with the gloves and a note that he'd touched the birds with the gloves so maybe don't use them for anything else. Then he went back to his cart.

The doors to Target had been easy enough to open since nothing was really holding them shut. He'd parked relatively close to the front, next to the handicap-spots, and briefly contemplated throwing a trashcan through the closed doors, before trying to simply slide the doors open. He wasn't even entirely surprised when that worked.

The lights were still out and he'd already prepared for the stench of the rotting foods with a face mask he swiped from the hospital. The smell still made his eyes water. He was thankful for the ambitious design of the store that'd placed huge skylights on the roof, running parallel with the isles so he didn't have to burn any more of the torch batteries.

Stepping in, he'd called out for anyone possibly lurking indoors, but it was clear from the stack of yellow grass and loose trash that'd blown up to the front doors, that no one had gone through them for a while. He didn't expect an answer and his expectations were met.

Cake stood at the canned goods isle with the empty cart. He eyed at the seemingly endless rows of rainbow-colored tin cans ranging from fruit to soup to fruit soup to entire canned animals. He picked up a can of pineapple and weighed it in his hand nervously.
"….Ok, I'm gonna loot you now! I'm sorry!" he shouted at the rafters.
"-*rry...*" they echoed back.
"I'm really gonna do it!" He glanced back down to the can, then around him, not really waiting for something to happen. Clouds drifted slowly over the skylight in perfect silence.
Cake carefully set the pineapple can in his shopping cart.
"I'm really looting now! Sorry!" He picked up another can but the empty store remained unmoved. "I've never done this before so... uh... I don't know why I'm saying this really!" He'd set a few more cans in the cart and each time he let go of one, it got a little easier. At least he'd have food.
He exhaled.
I don't think the pigeons care, son.
His posture mellowed in resignation.

And the ones inside are probably all dead anyway.

He pushed the cart forward, picked up a haul of tuna cans, then moved on to the candy aisle.

Cake had written a list of things he'd need before going in (mostly camping gear and food), but by the time he'd gone through it, things you generally didn't need on camping trips had appeared in his cart.

He'd stuck batteries in a Furby before he'd gotten to the checkout lane and it was chirping along merrily in the cart as he pushed them through the doors.

The cart was overflowing.

Cake set the Furby on the car roof giving a final hesitant glance at his loot all packed in the car. It wasn't his.

He felt a twitch on his side as his conscience gave him a very small but poignant kick. Angrily, he pulled open a M&Ms bag and stuffed a handful in his mouth. The sweets didn't taste much like anything at all, but he forced himself to continue chewing and swallowing long after there was any pleasure gained from eating them. Then he dropped the empty bag on the ground and stepped on it.

The Furby let out an appreciative squeal.

Cake glared at it, then huffed off to the driver's seat.

He felt sick from the candy and angry at everything. The anger sat on his shoulders and neck, playing at his muscles like a harp.

He hit the gas a little too hard and the Sedan jerked forward with a screech.

The city was disappearing in the rear view mirror and Cake felt his body starting to relax again. He'd gotten away with the goods. The further he got from Target, the more they started to feel like necessities, and less like a mass of stolen guilt weighing down the back end of the car.

Cake glanced in the side mirror. The last apartment building was just a white stripe on top of the green sea and then it disappeared when the road curved right.

He eased his foot off the gas and leaned back a little. The (newly acquired) Best Of American Authors CD droned steadily in the car player, and it almost felt like a regular road trip. Except for all the empty cars and trucks littering the road sides. And all the stuff in the car boot. And whatever he might find in New Port, because Cake had suspicions he was doing his best to pass off as useless paranoia.

He felt his neck tightening again and cranked the CD player up louder. He'd head for Talina first. Failing that, maybe Matt's? Matt had been good with his grandparents and their mutual circle of friends… Cake's thoughts trailer off. If he found Matt and Toni, they might have a baby. It'd be 5 years old. It would have adult words and bamboo-fiber leggings, and look like a shaved pudding-version of Matt and Toni. And he couldn't be mad at the baby for taking his room because it wasn't the baby that took it. He could only be mad at himself for calling the kid an it. And it had been 6 years. 6 years.

6 years and not a few days.

The directionless resentment settled on his forehead.

14.

The car purred along at an easy pace, dipping sometimes left, sometimes right, ducking the empty vehicles littering the road. Cake would slow down when antlers or flanks peeked through the foliage next to the road, and stop for a squirrel. More than once he'd have to back up, and go back to a smaller road when abandoned trucks or vans blocked the main road. An SUV parked sideways and he could just push it aside; the car would go tumbling down the side of the road, mowing down the tall grass as it ripped into the car's axles and grill. A tipped over van though? That meant another rickety byway, and another twenty minutes extra, eyes peeled hard on the undergrowth stretching its blades and branches towards the small strip of gray civilization running in the middle of it.

The roadsides were littered with empty husks; Dodgers and Beatles, SUVs and trucks. And an 18-wheeler on its side blocking the entrance to the cattle farm Cake had passed a few days before.

A few years before.

He had to keep reminding himself that it might be 2023, but his brain rebelled against the thought. Eventually he gave up. It didn't matter. It mattered where his family was. Where all the people who should've been driving these cars were.

A sweet, sulfury smell surged through the AC as he passed the 18-wheeler.

Eggs, Cake thought as his eyes glided over the axles and tires decorating the side of the truck. The pipes and hubcaps were washed clean from one side, like rain had passed over more than once and left the underside untouched. But the truck looked like it might's been going to the farm, not coming from it. Why would it be taking eggs to a farm? *How many eggs did farmers eat in a day anyway,* Cake thought idly, his brow scrunched up.

He'd driven a good mile already when the penny finally dropped; cows. No cows on the side of the road. No cows outside. That brown line between the green and the sky, with horns and moos and big friendly eyes, was missing.

The cows were probably still in there, weren't they?

Cake hit the breaks and the car squealed to a halt.

He drummed the steering wheel nervously staring at his thumbs. His heart was beating much too loudly again. Did he want to know?

Nothing was moving on the road. He couldn't see anyone in the mirror, though he didn't know what he'd expected. The road was an endless straight line stretching out behind him, spotted with empty cars in various states of repair.

His thumbs stopped in mid air, then twitched involuntarily. Cake shook his head and got out of the car.

There was a lead ball rolling around in his stomach. A hard, black lump in an empty space, pulling down the muscles around it. The sun was up, simmering the road and the cars, and birds sat silently in treetops tilting their heads.

Cake quickly hopped over to the other side of the road, still instinctively checking for oncoming traffic from both sides, before making good time jogging back to the truck. The truck didn't smell. He ran his hand along the side of the container as he passed around it, fingers gathering up black soot.

The main building of the farm stood square across the yard from the main gate. Cake headed there first and buzzed their doorbell his knuckles white. A glance through the windows revealed the same as with any other house he'd knocked on: dark rooms and lifeless furniture.

Cake turned back, crossing the enormous yard again, heading towards the long sheet metal buildings out back. Their domed roofs rose like snow castles in the green summery fields, supported by tractors and harrows and drags parked to the sides. He walked slower than he could have. The stench was making itself known and even though the terrible dread of certainty had attached itself to his feet, making them heavy and numb, he had to see for himself. He stopped in front of the small side door to the cow shed.

A tiny snake slithered away into the grass.

I need to...
He needed to reach for the door handle.
He needed to open the doors.

Cake closed his eyes as the wall of rotten stink fell through them.
He just had to know for sure.

The pens were filled with cattle in different stages of decomposing. Some were oozing out from under the pen doors, some had collapsed in on themselves. Some had expanded as their hides cracked from drought, making a map of fresh pink fractures in the brown fur.
Cake gagged and turned away to heave, trying to draw in fresh air, but there was none. The smell of rot had consumed it all. There was not one cow alive in there.
He threw up.
The sick mingled with the ooze that used to be cows under his feet and he threw up again, before realizing that he'd continue throwing up until he'd move away from the door.

Sitting under a tree at the other end of the farm, Cake wiped his eyes. Partially because of all the throwing up, partially because of the-... His mind stopped on its track and he pinched his eyes closed. The tree was solid behind his back, the ground dry between his fingers. These were good sensations to have, he thought, inhaling deeply, mostly through his mouth. A whiff of bile kept drifting up and he kept running his tongue over his teeth, wincing from the taste. His teeth were fuzzy. He hadn't washed them since the night at the gift shop and that was a good two days ago. Now he just felt too tired. His eyes started stinging again, the pressure building behind them as his cheeks flushed red. He could feel them burning as he tried wiping away the tears.

Dirt ground against his face. His hands were dirty. Cake quickly wiped them on his pants and let out a patchy sigh. He'd wanted to know and now he knew. That was all there was to it. He looked up at the leaves rustling above him. Further off a bird had boldly started chirping again.

He pushed himself up and headed back to the car, keeping his eyes on the sky and the road to avoid looking elsewhere. Not at the farm, not at the truck, just the brilliant blue sky reaching from one edge of the world to the other. He felt a little dizzy walking with his head cocked back.

A quiet baa sounded somewhere far behind him.

Cake stopped. He was starting to hear things.

Another baa. Two overlapping.

He was standing on the road eyes darting around, trying to distinguish between the empty cars and whatever might be moving between them.

Far in the distance he caught them; three sheep casually sauntering between the wrecks, being very round, soft and sheeply.

Cake rubbed his nose on the back of his hand. The whatever that was decomposing on the barn floor was still lingering in his mind, but there were alive sheep here and that was something. That was a good something. He decided not to open any more doors that stunk of death.

15.

By 5pm, the sun was starting to inch its way to a sunset and American Authors had long since changed to a collection of A Prairie Home Companion. The familiar puns, fake adverts, the bubbly conversation had cheered Cake up. Oregon wasn't that far away and Talina would know. Know people, know the news. Everything would be just fine, Cake thought and a flash of chocolate milkshake drifted through his mind. Sure everything looked bleak and dead now, but that was just Idaho and the day sure was beautiful.

The car started making a noise unlike cars in motion needed to make.

It whirred, then fell silent as the gas pedal went limp. Cake stomped it a few times without making a difference. The speed dropped on its own and slowly the Sedan glided to a halt.

He stared at the fuel gauge anger boiling behind his eyes. *Really? Really.* He slammed the wheel and let out a frustrated growl. "Seriously? You're gone for 6 years and forget to top up?!" He slapped himself on the forehead leaving a visible hand print.

Ow.

Cake rubbed his forehead.

He tumbled out of the car forehead throbbing, and popped the trunk open. The

158

Walmart-appropriated backpack balanced peacefully right on top of everything. Grabbing it, he threw a few water bottles and candy bars in for the road. The spare canister had to be jiggled out from under the pile. He hesitated for a moment with the empty canister in his hand. There was a gas station a few miles back and it probably had an emergency generator, but--

He sucked on his teeth thoughtfully, then pulled out the heavy duty bolt cutters he'd picked up at the store, and stuffed them in the backpack. The handles poked out like ancient melee weapons.

A fixed blade hunting knife was glinting in the setting sun, stuffed next to the loot. Cake eyed it for a moment. He'd taken it in case he'd need to build a fire or gut a fish, but the woods were starting to cast longer shadows and there might be strings to cut and ghouls to stab. He let out a nervous guffaw. *No such thing as ghouls in the woods. Ghouls aren't real. Ghouls are hungry goth rockers.*

The woods are just dark, he repeated.

And there were no street lights.

He glanced at the darkness under the trees. A pair of large, luminescent eyes flashed in the treeline and quickly disappeared. Cake grabbed the knife, wrapping the sheath around his ankle. There were things with more sharp teeth than he had, ambling in the shadows.

He slammed the trunk shut with conviction. The metal on metal on insulation boomed from tree to tree like it was the only sound in existence, stirring up birds that'd just settled in for the evening. They circled high above him croaking disapprovingly.

Cake started back down the highway muttering to himself. If he only knew how to steal gasoline from a car, he wouldn't have to walk far. The road was littered with them, every 500 feet harboring a new make and a model, or two.

But he'd never been into sabotaging other people's cars, and he couldn't check online, so he lacked both the skill and tools for proper fuel thievery, and somehow this idea was only slightly less frustrating than having to walk back two miles while the sun's last rays disappeared behind the horizon. A truly pitch black night would settle over the world.

Cake kicked loose leaves deigning to blow directly onto his path. The woods rustled. He glared at the leaves on his feet and in the trees. "Whaddaya looking at," he spat at them. The trees groaned back.

But it wasn't the trees.

It came from ahead, down the road.

Another groan. It came from a deep belly, through a sharp nose and sharper teeth. And it was followed by the click click click of claws on asphalt. All these things he could hear with disturbing accuracy as Cake stared down a gigantic black bear hovering between two cars just a few feet ahead.

16.

"Oh no..."

The grizzly stood up to its full height forming a mountain of damp fur and teeth between the cars. It let out an ear-shattering growl. This wasn't a warning. This was a statement of intent. Drool had matted around its mouth and every move the bear made gushed forth a cloud of rotten meat and musk.

"Hold up," Cake's hands flew up instinctively as the bear bared its teeth.

Bad move bad move bad move shit shit shit.

He tried crouching down slowly.

"Hey now," Cake spoke as softly as he could. "I'll get out of your way. Not here to cause trouble," he continued in a hushed, reassuring tone, touching one hand to the ground for balance.

The bear groaned and flashed its entire maw. A stench of dead things, dirt and blood filled the air.

"No no, buddy. You don't want me," Cake kept trying. At the same time his free hand was reaching for the bolt cutters and pulling them to the front as slowly as he could. "I'm not tasty. I'm bitter. Yeah. I'm very bitter on the inside-,"

The bear lunged towards him and swung one giant paw at the bolt cutters that went flying in an arch over the side of the road and disappeared into the grass.

There was now nothing between them, and the bear slumped forwards pink mouth filled with fangs and pain gaping at his head.

Cake ducked putting his weight on the hand on the ground and swung the opposing foot towards the bear's knee. Or as close as he could guess where a bear's knees were. It connected with something that gave a tiny squeak and the bear came tumbling towards him. He grabbed handfuls of fur, his fingers sinking in the loose skin like there was nothing but folds and hunger under the coat, until they reached something solid enough, then yanked back, putting all his weight on the foot still firmly planted on the ground. The bear flew over him in an angry arch of fur while Cake rolled on his back and landed back down on his feet on the asphalt, facing the two cars. The bear hit the ground behind him with a satisfying thud.

He glanced back. The bear was momentarily confused about the change in location. But it was by no means out of the game. His pride in a move well executed quickly evaporated as the bear rolled back up and found him staring. A single bloodied eye glared back at him from the black mass, and the teeth revealed themselves in a grim, murderous grin.

"Oh boy," Cake breathed as he flipped back to face the bear. His hands flailed about in the dusk, looking for anything. The bolt cutters were long gone and the road had nothing but leaves and pebbles to offer.

His fingers brushed on the knife hilt.

The bear made a lunge, throwing its entire weight towards him in a wall of muscle and ravenous hunger piling down, as Cake pulled the knife, weighed the blade and evened out the imbalance without thinking, hurtled it towards the animal billowing towards him. A black tide reached over him and all he could see was teeth and tongue and fur and...

Then nothing.

***

Cake could smell blood. He could smell all kinds of things that were dead, and things that were rank and wet and had never known neither shampoo nor tooth brush. Wet things on his face and dirt on his skin.

He pushed up and rolled to his side, and the bear corpse slid off him. A thousand pounds of loose flesh and bone in a fur bag sagged to the asphalt. He could see the sky. Lying on the road, wisps of clouds drifted above him, slow and content.

His arms were bloodied, but as Cake wiped them with the t-shirt, nothing seemed to be broken. His skin was intact, the blood wasn't his. He looked at the black heap cooling next to him.

He'd hit the bear squarely between the eyes and the knife had sink in to the hilt. A good 5 inches of metal had just burrowed into the animal's skull and severed whatever it needed.

A red pool was slowly seeping under them. Cake brushed wet off the side of his face. Mostly blood, probably some spit too. All nicely mingled, so it hardly mattered. Neither was something he wanted on his face. He was shaking. He didn't even know why. His hands were perfectly calm but a cold rush ran through his back and core. How did he do that? It felt so natural. Cake rubbed his fingertips together in front of his face, then made a fist. His hand looked normal. But his normal hand could just kill a bear?

The carcass was so much heavier without life in it. Wiggling out from under it took more time than he expected, and by the time Cake was on his feet, the sky was a dark teal with echoes of stars.

He put his foot on the bear's skull and yanked the knife out. It came with chunks and a sputter of blood.

"I don't....," he muttered, "skulls are soft?"

He looked around the road and zoomed in on an empty car's side mirror. The blade felt light in his had as it flipped around easily, landed between his fingers and then took off into the mirror in one smooth movement. He'd hit the mirror and the knife struck through it sticking in the plastic. The mirror shards cascaded to the ground.

"Uhm, ok. That's 7 years of bad luck." He pursed his lips into a tight line as the misjudgment sunk in. But he felt confident he'd proven a point about knife-throwing.

Hours later, the night was a cool blue. Cake was staring up at the stars at the Shell-station in amazement. He'd never seen so many. Not even when camping.

He'd had to walk back a good hour of driving and frankly, the stars were the only thing making him feel not scared for his life right now. So he focused on those. How big the sky was. How everything was a weird, cold shade of dark, completely unlike in all the bad movies where they tried making a day-for-night shots with a blue filter over the lens. He'd never realized how much light the Moon and the stars really shone until there was no other light to compete with them, nor trees to cover the sky.

The gas station was as empty and creepy as the rest of the town behind it. There was no music echoing from the distance, no voices of friends hanging out. No hum from the constant traffic, no low buzz from neon lights. There were just bugs, occasionally whizzing by him, and bats squeaking at each other high up. Cake breathed in the night.

He circled around the back of the station to find the emergency generator and kept his fingers crossed the tank had gasoline in it to run. The lock snapped open easily with the bolt cutters and the start button was mercifully easy to locate as the only button in the middle of the dashboard that was readily reachable.

He tapped the knob and the generator churred alive scaring away rats sleeping under it. Suddenly the night was less silent, as the metallic hum of the generator surrounded the station.

The switch board was easy enough to find in the same place it was on the models he was familiar with. Cake flipped the power on. Lights flickered in the gas pumps, blinking from a deep slumber, then lighting up as they awakened. It was at the same time inviting and disheartening. The shadows around the pumps deepened as the chugging of the generator rolled over the flat fields and flat houses and clung to the few trees around them. It felt like the only sound in the world and like it didn't belong anymore. This place belonged to the bats, the rats and the night. Electricity was an invader to the peaceful balance.

Cake filled his canister and another he'd sneaked from inside, silently following moths gather around the lights, bumping against them and each other. He could make out the flutter of the wings and the stops and starts of flight patterns. The soft bodies tumbling on his head when the competition for the light got vicious.

He sighed at the canister.

The night rushed over the gas station again as he turned off the emergency generator. No sense in leaving it running on the off chance some other poor sap would drive this way and need a gallon or two. It wasn't going to make the milk at the convenience store uncurdle, the sweet smell disappear.

The now-familiar emptiness filled his ears again.

Cake rubbed his chin looking out from inside the station. "Getting to midnight," he mused looking at the wall clock behind the station counter ticking away loyally. Thankfully batteries didn't care about the absence of people.

"Since I'm staying..." He rummaged around behind the till and the back room, looking for something to sleep on, but only found jackets and t-shirts. He arranged them on the floor, after dusting away dirt and bugs, as far away from the cold storage units as possible.

Round eyes stared at his moving shape through the window as he scoured through the gas station. He caught a glimpse of the something looking straight at him, two glowing discs in the pitch black night, and swung his torch at them. An owl took off, unimpressed by the spotlight.

As he curled on the floor for the night, in his makeshift bed, Cake could swear he heard a howl somewhere outside.

The knife he placed on the floor next to his head.

17.

Of the three Pringles cans he'd arranged on different surfaces, none survived. He'd hit them all.

Cake picked up the Cheesy Dip one and was very impressed how accurately he'd hit the blobby white face between the eyes with a pencil. He didn't think he'd even aimed that time. Yet the hunting knife, the pencil and the plastic fork had all found their targets with surprising accuracy. He was particularly impressed by the plastic fork since it was a flimsy, light-weight thing just a breath above a spork, and with no balance to it whatsoever. He was almost sure physics wasn't supposed to act this way.

Wanting to test another theory, he grabbed a selection of things that weren't meant for throwing, which turned out surprisingly hard since most things at a convenience stores weren't meant for it. He had to think particularly hard about things that really, *really*, weren't meant for it and should not be able make any sort of distance. An inflatable neck pillow was one, magazines and plastic spoons another. He hauled his hoard to the side of the field and looked at a farm house catching the early rays of the sun a good half a mile away. He grabbed a magazine

168

and chucked it. It took flight, but instead of gliding over the field, the pages took wind and shot the paper projectile high up past the electric wires where a stronger current grabbed it, and it disappeared into the blue flapping like an airborne emu.

Cake stood watching it with his jaw hanging open.

"Ok, so we physics?" he said reaching down for the inflatable pillow.

He leaned back with the pillow in his hand angling vaguely in the direction of the farm house. "Jesus, wouldn't that be something…" He flung the U-shaped pillow as hard as he could and heard a distant thud as it exploded against the barn wall.

Cake blinked.

He looked down at his right palm, turning his hand over slowly and running his fingers along his perfectly normal human skin. The veins looked human and so did the hair and the pores, but the throwing sure wasn't something human arms (or physics) should allow. He traced the edges of the circular burn mark on his shoulder. *Maybe I'm part robot now…. Someone drugged me and stole my arm and toes and now I'm part bionic?*

He wiggled his toes in deep thought for a moment, then picked up the spoons with his left hand and flung them at the farm in a bundle. There were distant thuds as the spoons struck through the wood paneling on the side of the building.

Maybe I have two bionic arms? I could be a robot… he stared into the middle distance a little unsure as to how to feel about possibly being a robot.

Abruptly, he spun on his heels and headed back to the convenience store with a determined frown on his face. They had to have something that he could use to test things out.

The magnets he picked up didn't seem to do anything. They just rolled around in his hand and repelled each other and he was no more dexterous in juggling with them as he had been at any other point in his life. They rippled here, there and everywhere, not attaching themselves to his hand or his feet, and rolled under shelves. He bent down trying to reach them, but no magnetic waves attracted them to his hand from the far corners of the store, so the magnets remained in their hiding places.

He took a fresh hunting knife from a display cage and poured some antibacterial hand wash on it, hoping it would do the same as any sanitizing liquid, and poked his finger with it. A small but persistent stream of blood came gushing out and he started feeling faint. If he was a robot, he was a very well programmed robot as he felt nausea and there was a lot of that Terminator-type human skin structure over his metallic bones. If the bleeding reaction was simulated, it was extraordinarily accurate to real life, as it was really making him feel ill.

Cake sat down feeling lightheaded. He stuck his hand up, finger wrapped in toiletpaper, and reflected how this experiment might not have been the best idea. While waiting, his eyes wandered around the store fixating on the lighters and he remembered how the only thing that really exposed the metallic endoskeleton in the movie, had been fire.

He blinked rapidly, then discarded the idea.

Maybe he could just make the best of being a machine, if he had metallic parts buried between his human parts. Accept, adapt, overcome. He had a weird arm or two now. This was the new reality. No people in Idaho, just super strong robot arms.

Cake stared at his non-bleeding hand as his resolved hardened unlike fudge should. He'd be the best human robot. If his programming wanted him to kill specific people, he'd try to resist it. *If thine surprise robot hand offends thee...*

Cake tapped at his eyelids. His eyeballs felt squishy under the lids. Maybe his vision was still human as it wasn't a machine-like red and no numbers flashed before his eyes like in the movies. And he couldn't see any better than before. From what he remembered. If they were robot eyes designed to be squishy and non-enhanced, then he surely wouldn't be a very good killer robot. This felt like a comforting idea.

In the back of his mind an errand thought whispered *"but what if you've always been a robot..."*

The bleeding finally stopped and Cake bandaged up his hand.

If he could throw things with inhuman accuracy and force, and he could do flips to ward off attacking bears, could he do something else too that he didn't know about yet?

He was absentmindedly staring at a gun rack as the thought skipped through his brain; can I shoot a gun?

He'd never been interested in anything but laser guns, but then again, he'd paid even less attention to knives growing up, so it wasn't an impossible thought that he'd now have skills he hadn't thought of as useful in his teens.

Cake picked up a rifle from the wall. It was wooden and metallic and he held it a little awkwardly like asking his hands "now what?". He put the riffle back. The handguns were under a glass and the throbbing in his finger reminded him that he would definitely still bleed, a lot, if he just tried smashing through that. The display firearms were given a pass.

There had to be a handgun somewhere around here he could try...

No handguns were under the checkout desks or in the back rooms, just another riffle hidden behind a filing cabinet in one of the offices. Cake moved outside and eyed at the few cars standing empty at the station lot.

All of the cars were unlocked. The first one just had bills stuffed in its glove compartment, with mint tobacco and a pack of Trojans. The mint made Cake's eyes water. He backed away quickly wiping his face.

The second one had a broken tail light, and a bobblehead Virgin Mary. It also did, indeed, have a handgun in a little black polyester holster hidden in a potato chip bag on the front seat. The holster was slippery with grease. The gun itself smelled only vaguely like potatoes.

Cake pulled the gun out of the holster very carefully.

It was small and black and angular, and felt much heavier than he'd thought. It was also cold even now in the middle of the day. Cake tried gripping it with confidence. His fingers fumbled how to manage their way around the trigger. It seemed small. Like made for children. He had a horrified realization that the gun could've been designed to fit a child's hands.

"My fingers must've gotten bigger in the past 6 years," he mumbled nervously to push the idea out of his head.

As soon as the words slipped out of his mouth, a calming denial washed over him. Yes, it must've been his fingers that got big. Not the gun that was made for children.

He eventually managed to find a grip that seemed almost balanced and landed the tip of his index finger on the trigger. The farm house still seemed like a comfortably far off target that he wouldn't hit anything important, though guilt nudged at his belly for all the spoons now embedded in the barn wall.

He pointed the gun straight on, but it felt... wrong. Unnatural.

He tried aiming it sideways, loosely balancing the weight on his thumb. The position felt equally off. The trigger was heavy and immobile. Cake closed his eyes, protecting his face with his free hand as he tried pulling it, without success. The trigger remained still. He shook the gun in frustration. Nothing. Not a spiff or a spittle.

He let his arm relax and drop to his side; "I have no idea what I'm doing here." The baby-gun was a useless lump weighing down his fingers.

In a moment of inspiration, Cake grabbed the gun by the barrel and chucked it out in the field as far as he could. In the distance he could hear metal on tile as the gun cracked on the chimney of the farm house and a loud bang echoed over the field. The neon light circling the gas station roof shattered to pieces right behind him raining yellow and red shards around the tanks, like a magic circle warding off anyone trying to steal gasoline.

In the distance, the chimney toppled in slow motion, first a few a tiles bouncing off the roof, then all of them folding into a pile of dust and wreckage next to the side of the building.

Oops

Cake hid the empty holster in a trash can next to the station and carefully arranged all the envelopes, wires and plastic bags back into their places in the car, while eyeing guiltily at the bobblehead Mary, before making sure the car doors closed properly.

He filled his backpack with candy bars, canned foods, and water bottles, and started back into the direction he'd left his car.

18.

The papers in the little red notebook were starting to show their age. They were curling from the edges and grease stains had patched the sides translucent.

Cake pulled out a gel pen, scribbled a few letters before noticing whatever kind of gel had been in it had run dry. He threw the pen into his little makeshift garbage bag and pulled out a new one from a box of 20 he'd repossessed from OfficeMax in Salina Cruz. The word "repossessing" made him feel more at ease whenever he walked out with a bag full of things without paying. This was redistribution of wealth in its rawest form. There were necessary supplies. He had a necessity. So he took the supplies. That was his mantra.

It didn't stop him from somehow breaking into sweat right around the door alarms, though. This, he realized, was a completely unnecessary fear as there was no electricity. No electricity, no guards, no guard dogs, no clerks running after him, no customers staring at him accusingly.

But the fear of security checks and accidentally stealing something was a primal one.

He flicked the rubber ball off the tip of the pen, and continued writing. A number and a location in big, block letters:

371, CLOSE TO WYTHEVILLE

He set the pen aside and pulled out a parachute flare from his backpack. Holding it as far away from his body as he could, Cake aimed high above the trees. The safety came off, he pulled the cord and the flair went up with a tail of red smoke.

He stayed looking up as the flare disappeared from sight then suddenly burst into a bright red star, slowly floating down, glimmering danger, intruder, between the Moon and the pinpricks in the night. The sky remained the same. It never cared for emergency flares, red or white, or emergencies in general. The real, natural stars looked down on the red impostor as it slowly faded from sight.

Cake sat down next to the bonfire and started scribbling down on the notebook again.

The fire crackled unrushed. It warmed his face and dyed the surrounding trees deep orange. A halo of familiarity surrounded him and his camper van as his beans sizzled merrily in a can by the fire. He'd set a flat stone at the edge of it, scrubbed the paper off the tin and popped it open, before setting it on the stone to heat up the beans inside. It almost felt like camping.

If the camping was forever and you couldn't make it stop.

The beans bubbled.

Cake looked up from his notebook and pursed his lips. An echo of resignation grabbed at his chest, but he shook it off. *Beans are perfectly fine. There's nuts and fruit in the morning. Beans are... just. Fine.*

He pulled on an oven mitt and poured the beans on a plate and inhaled. He added a small note in his book:

STOCK DIFFERENT BEANS
MAYBE NOT BEANS

A little pepper and dry crackers and it wasn't bad. It was a meal. It was the same meal he'd had most nights with the slight variation of soy sausages a few months ago, but still.

The flames danced gleefully as Cake put on a CD of a radio play he'd found. The player he'd picked up worked on batteries, so he tried not using it all the time, but this had become a routine. Listening to a play, slowly chewing on the beans and waiting to dig into the cup of instant coffee and candy he had reserved for desert, making notes of the last city he scoped out in his notebook.

His teeth ached mildly.

He'd drawn a simple map of the main streets and marked the service stations and grocery stores he'd seen on his drive through so he'd have something to use as landmarks when he'd go in the next day by foot. Then he'd drawn himself as a little smiling stick figure roughly where he'd set up camp.

The smile was important. Seeing a little smile like that made him feel less lonely, just like listening to the ghost voices on the radio talking about things that had very little meaning anymore. Not that he thought everyone on the CDs he had were dead, just that the radio play was from 1956, so it was likely that those actors might be dead by 2023.

20-...24.

He looked at the number on the notebook.

The beans started tasting mostly like can.

There really wasn't a nice way around it after over 350 days of eating a lot of beans and dry crackers. It was still over 350 days.

Cake sighed wistfully at the thought of the beef and cheese manicotti he'd had in the early days. And hamburgers. Even a whole chicken! It would never cease to amaze him what people had managed to stick in cans. But as the days wore on, the sell-by dates on the cans passed and he became more and more reluctant to test if he could still eat the beef in the dusty, dented cans bulging out of their seams.

Cans that were round in every direction, he'd learned, were not cans he should open.

He absentmindedly rubbed a scar on his forehead like it'd just appeared there.

No, stay away from cans that didn't look like cans.

Over a year ago, he'd gotten to Newport without much more trouble from bears. The bear carcass was already half eaten by the time he got back to his car. Buzzards were picking through the thick fur and looked at him disapprovingly as he tried to pass them discreetly to get to his car. There were bloody paw prints on the asphalt, which meant other animals had been there to take their share.

The bear had looked much smaller half eaten, than when it was alive. Smaller and deflated. Internal organs added up surprising bulk to a body, he'd learned.

The closer to Newport he had gotten, the more empty cars littered the highway. The good thing with highways though, was how wide they were. More space for him to slip past and he didn't have to stop nearly as often.

But a dread had crept in.

More empty cars, more seagulls screeching overhead and rabbits and badgers wandering along the street. It looked like they were going to see a show, taking over the highways en masse like that. When he passed them, they would quickly bounce back into the woods or the fields, but would poke out again as soon as his car was a dozen feet away.

When he passed the first bus stop, he saw a handbag on the ground.

He would see many handbags on the ground driving down the streets. Almost as many as there were walking aids, cell phones, and even guns next to vacant cop cars. Just discarded. The cars were rained on several times, with thick water streaks coloring them ashen, and bird droppings spotting them white and green. It was almost as if the birds had taken vengeance on them once they saw they could do it without recourse.

Grass had started to sprout from the sides of the buildings and from cracks in the pavement. And over everything hung that strange sweet smell that was almost like a good cheese, but in the wrong way.

He'd gone to every address. Every friend. Then every relative. No one was home. Every store stood dark and silent. Doors were open and electronic devices littered the streets, but no lights burned and no voices answered when he hollered. Half eaten meals sat on restaurant tables, cars leaned head first against street lights and building walls, charred facades speckled otherwise pristine rows of commercial buildings.

Talina's bakery wasn't where it should've been. In her spot stood an empty Starbucks. Cake could see the impressive mold collection in the display case instead of fresh baked goods. *Freshly baked? That does look like some fresh penicillin!* he'd thought then hung his head. It was a pretty bad pun even for him. Susan's Sweets' sign had moved a block, to the other side of the road. It was over one of those invisible lines, the lines that arbitrarily divided a city so that one block was a good and wealthy and desirable place to live, but the building right next to it was not. He'd shrugged and thought that it still wasn't a terrible place as any of the hipsters clients would probably just enjoy slumming it on the 'wrong side of the town'... which was about two feet from the 'right side of the town'.

The door had been unlocked but as soon as he stepped in, a wave of cockroaches dispersed over the floor like a ripple in a pond.

The decor was the same, save for new lamp shades. But no people. Just a lot of mold and roaches and dust.

From Susan's Sweets, he'd gone to his old home, or his home-that'd-been-his-home-right-up-until-possible-phantom-babies, but all the doors inside were locked and the corridors dark and empty. He knocked on doors and the knocks echoed like the last sound in the universe, then quickly died out.

He'd sat a while on the entrance of the building looking at the sun setting behind other buildings and only heard crickets. No lights lit up anywhere. The street lights had cobwebs catching the last rays of the sun and a few large cocoons strung in them like the spiders had started Christmas decorating early.

No one was here to help him. Where ever they'd evacuated the people from Idaho, they'd also taken the people in Newport.

He'd leaned his face in his hands as the dread he'd suppressed now spread its long fingers round his heart and shoved it up his throat. He just wanted to talk to someone. Anyone. Anyone who had the slightest idea where everyone was and maybe also why he could throw knives and bears because those were things that confused him. But not as much as the missing everyone.

He had to find someone.

After a long night laying on a couch in a Target (it was a nice, burgundy couch. He'd picked it based on the kind he'd always wanted but could never afford), he'd hatched a plan. The plan had two parts:
1. find people
2. find mom and Brutus and Talina and all the people in his group chat. Even the ones he didn't like.

He was satisfied with this. Small steps. First any people. Then the important people. Then someone could tell him what he'd been doing with his hands for the past 6 years. Then someone could explain what happened to the 6 years in general.

He'd had breakfast in the dried food isle and packed up the Sedan with anything he found useful, including a bag of batteries and the CD-player. He picked up two new knives, just in case he'd lose one or would have to stab two things at once.

Holding a knife had a strangely reassuring effect on him. He'd find people. As long as he had a knife in his hand, he'd find anyone.

Before noon he was already heading down to Portland. It seemed like the best place to start, being the largest city anywhere near Newport.

Portland had been equally empty, but instead of handbags and cell phones, there were kickboards strewn along the sidewalks. After Portland he stuck to the coast line, making small detours as he'd made his way south, checking out whatever larger facilities and suburbs he saw signs to. California had palm trees. He'd picked fresh oranges from a farm near the road and for once didn't feel that guilty about taking something that he technically didn't pay for. Fresh fruit had tasted amazing after a week on rice and vitamin pills. He'd parked behind the Hollywood sign to draw a little outline of the main roads in his notebook and started counting days. It seemed like a fun little calendar-like thing to do since Cake had no real way of telling what day or even month it was. It was sunny. He was in California. He suspected most days there would be warm and sunny. The notes would help him track exactly which of those warm and sunny days it was.

The beach boulevards were empty aside from seagulls. He'd filled up his gas canisters and moved on, crossing over the abandoned border in Tijuana, then touring all the way to the tip and back and continuing on south following the ocean the best he could.

With maps he'd pick up whenever he'd cross a larger city, he could see a little further ahead, but he'd still had to back up and take a different route when the road would be blocked by vans or trees or natural disasters. Highways would disappear. They were marked on maps, but water or fire or rocks had come and taken them away. There was nothing he could do. Sometimes it was roads, sometimes entire cities, covered in seaweed, scum and dead fish, the buildings ripped apart by wind, water or fire, thrown against each other, rearranged into bricks or ashes.

The temperatures started getting humid and the crackers he'd stocked up on got softer. The candy bars just melted in their wrappers and licking the packaging clean left the better part of the food in his beard. He'd trimmed the beard to keep it out of his limited supply of candy bars.

He'd stop by beaches when he found them and took long baths, enjoying the privacy for a moment, until his guilt about enjoying his privacy overwhelmed him. Then he'd head back to his car, with salt water on his skin, and write in the notebook things that made him feel better while listening to a calming CD. Somewhere between Lima and Santiago he'd stopped listening to the calming CDs. It felt like overkill. It wasn't like he was bothered by the traffic noises or office deadlines. More rock music appeared in his car. The weather got colder and the air very thin. Gas stations were few and far between. After Puerto Montt, the Sedan broke down on a narrow road flanked by short, thick trees with tiny leaves like fir needles. He'd packed what he could and walked for days, sleeping sometimes in the field in his inflatable tent, or on the couches of abandoned farmhouses, with dinners and breakfasts half eaten and dried on their tables. He'd tried approaching some of the horses he'd seen running wild, but they were, rightfully, suspicious of him. He had no riding experience, but his foot hurt and the prosthesis had started to wear on him, so he'd put it in his backpack and stuffed a sock into the tip of his shoe. This had caused an entirely new kind of irritation, so he eventually discarded that too.

After week of sleeping roughly and being shunned by horses, he'd reached the next larger town. He'd settled there for a few days of sleeping in dusty beds and looking for cars that would still have gas in their tank. The more days passed, the more the cars would turn into rusty junk, with empty tanks and squirrels, cats and birds freely nesting in their empty bodies. He'd found a polka-dotted van with a chihuahua-sticker on the hood and a crunchy stick shift, and then spent a day cracking open gas tanks and sheds to cobble together a full tank and two emergency canisters. Spreading his sleeping bag at the back of the van he'd felt a renewed joy at having a mobile roof over his head and decided to amend his priority list to finding a good camper van as soon as he could. Van first, then people.

He wouldn't find people in South America.

He found nature taking over cities, inch by inch. Sometimes it was monkeys, following him around and being unnervingly human. He'd shouted after them a number of times, mistaking them for children in the dark, and then throwing rocks at them when they pulled the curtains off his Chilean van. The animals clearly didn't mind people disappearing as much as he did.

Mostly though, it was cats, rats, and large snakes.

Sometimes it was a flash of green light somewhere in his peripheral vision and something like wind (it WAS wind, right?) that almost sounded like speech. But never people.

Cake had stayed in South America until the next spring and then when the roads were clear again, he'd driven through Canada. Even in the early spring, the driving was slow as he'd never really thought of how much snow snowplows actually removed from the streets. Now it'd just stayed there and by June was slowly making it's way from ice to bare asphalt. He'd 'found' a newer camper van in Canada and taken to camping outside each city for a few days, sending up emergency flares, just in case he'd somehow managed to just miss another human while walking through a city with his megaphone.

He hadn't met anyone yet.

But he felt strongly like someone was there. It just stood to reason someone would be.

***

Cake sent out the second flare and sat sipping on his coffee, watching the flare fade into the night as it drifted down over the tree tops. Instant coffee, he was sure, was something he'd

187

love until the world *really* ended. It was a comforting piece of modern convenience, almost as good as anything from a chain store (or even better) and would never, ever, go off. When the world would truly end, he'd still have instant coffee.

Cake stared at the little bubbles floating on top of his coffee. He wasn't happy thinking about the possible end of the world. This paucity of people, this was just a glitch. A temporary situation. He'd fix it if he could just find the right button. Turn everything on again. He'd need to find someone to tell him where the buttons were.

The actors in the radio-play where having a moment. The piano swell behind the dialogue and between the sighs, there was a sloppy wet sound. A chill ran down his back as he remembered what it was like to kiss people. He hoped he'd never been that loud.

A low howl carried over the tree tops somewhere in the distance.

He'd heard the same howl, or at least a very similar one if not the exact same one, a few nights ago, and decided that sleeping inside the van was better even if he'd rather enjoy the camp fire outside. Nature was becoming very indifferent to his technological advantages and he'd found his tent, backpack or clothes mauled more than once after leaving them out of his sight.

Cake poured a shovel of sand on the camp fire. The trees around him fell dark as the flames sputtered and the fire turned to smoke. He jammed the notebook under his arm and climbed into the van coffee cup in one hand. All the other lights were turned off but the small reading light next to the bed. He laid down, exhaling deeply. Chest sinking, muscles relaxing, his body welcomed the crisp blankets. Aside from the loneliness, it was almost nice. His very own island of books and electricity and other normal human things. The van he'd picked had brand new - at the time of installation - solar panels attached to the roof, awarding him the luxury of ceiling lights and hot water.

He picked up a comic book he'd been browsing from the side table and settled in, flipping through it for a few minutes before he'd get too sleepy. Tomorrow was going to be another day of shouting at walls in yet another city, he thought, pushing his shoe off with his toes while staring intently at Calvin and Hobbes playing monsters.

A long guttural howl echoed over the trees outside the camp, this time much closer than before. The ground started trembling.

19.

Cake rushed outside pulling on his jacket. The trembling reverberated in a repeating pattern along the trees, shuddering leaves to the ground. A thud and a silence, a louder thud and a silence, leaves rustling against each other like crisp leather, tree trunks moaning in the distance before giving up and breaking in twain with brittle pops. The thuds landed closer with each second.

Cake looked up to the sky and saw the tree line thinning. Something plowed through it like a shark fin in water.

A final thud juddered him off his feet. He landed sharply on his tailbone as tree splinters rained down from above.

A mountain loomed over him.

It had huge paw-like feet, wider than the tree trunks it'd just crushed, disappearing under a cloak of long fur, that narrowed up to a tip above the tree tops. Vines ran around the trunk-like legs, blossoming in the cracks that might've been layers of hardened skin or actual bark. Cake was blinking rapidly. His brain was trying to decipher what it was seeing in the dark, just at the edge of the light shining from the camper. It made no sense in rational terms that a mountain would've just appeared next to his camp site. Walked there

190

with its own feet. Mountains didn't have feet, he was pretty sure.

It looked like cousin It, Cake though. If cousin It was huge. And had giant paws. And hands.

Hands.

A hand was reaching down towards him, pushing ahead of it a front of musky, warm air filled with dirt and earth and moss and caves and things that lived under rocks in those caves. Cake clambered backwards, trying to pedal out of the way. A futile effort since the hand was so large he would've had trouble out-running it, much less crab-walking backwards.

He braced himself, protecting his head with his arm… but the hand never touched him.

Cake opened his eyes and saw the hand hovering a few feet above him. He could hear his heart thumbing uncomfortably in his chest, physically too close to his rib cage. And he could hear something else.

A chattering.

A rhythmic chattering and gnashing. Like sharp teeth grinding against each other. Chitter. Chatter. Gnash. The sound pierced through his ear drums and send that uncommon feeling of revulsion through him, like nails on a chalk board.

The furry mountain remained still, seemingly fixed on something in the treeline past the little opening Cake had been camping in.

He turned to look at the sound.

And he wish he hadn't.

The moon was lighting up the opening casting a dim circle where details blurred and the edge of the trees was just a black wall and yet, in that wall, something was moving. It was gnashing its teeth. Cake was sure it was universally a bad thing when anything gnashed its teeth.

The shadows shifted forwards and figures started to emerge. It looked like the night was condensing, taking form in the moonlight as it moved forward. Before it was just a sound, but in the light, it had arms and heads and beaks and teeth. Four arms, skeletal and almost bare bone, with long talons at the ends. The talons moved in ticks, like they were mechanical. The bodies were wide and glinting. Feathered. The dark feathers grew in shapes that looked vaguely like armor. Between the thick feathers, a giant bird head, worn almost down to a skull. Teeth jutting out from the beaks, glinting wet. The teeth ground together. That's where the chattering was coming from; they were talking to each other. Or talking to Cake and the mountain. Making sounds that made him want to vomit. Cake pulled a terrified face involuntarily as the gnashing penetrated deeper through to his skull. If the shape of the bird things hadn't already been deeply terrifying, their sounds were wet chalk scratching directly on his brain.

The birds were monstrous in size. No wings, just talons and beaks and no legs. They hovered a foot off the ground, as more of them materialized from the darkness. A row of glistening beaks, like soldiers, talons tick tick ticking towards them.

Cake shook himself. The revulsion was turning his stomach. There was something so inherently wrong in the creatures, it was making him panic. He screwed his eyes shut and forced himself to roll to the left, to get out from under the hand. When he opened his eyes, the birds were standing next to his camper. Did they just appear there? Had they moved? Did they want him or the mountain? The gnashing turned to whispers. The most terrifying whispers he'd ever heard. Moist and sharp, something he didn't so much hear as he felt at the back of his head.

"Flesh..."

Why was any of this intelligible to him? They could've been saying anything. No, his brain was just leaping to conclusions.

The birds scraped their talons along the back of his camper van. *"Not... flesh..."*

The birds needed to stop talking. He didn't need to know. He didn't want to know. He just wanted away from them.

Cake crouched down and tried moving towards the open door without drawing attention to himself. Most of the birds seemed to be surrounding the furry creature, locked in anticipation, both unsure who would make the first move.

Cake didn't know what anyone's first move would be, but he was almost positive it wouldn't be good. The three creatures examining his camper were dripping something to the ground. It smelled sweet.

He made another careful shift towards the door, shoes and breath intolerably loud.

The birds stopped. They swiveled their heads towards him, like the necks didn't have joints at all. The heads were just a loose decoration on top of rotting feathers. The empty sockets bored down on him and Cake could feel sweat beads running down his back. It was a Mexican stand off with eyeless demons. The chattering and movement had all stopped. Even air hung perfectly still.

Cake slowly let his eyelids droop, then close, feeling the night shift around him as things materialized next to his skin...

... and he jumped. Eyes closed, he lunged at the camper door and landed on the floor barely missing claws that hooked themselves on the door frame. He rolled around and kicked at the skeletal arms, shattering two. The bird creature let out a wail and he could see the dark red underside of its tongue poking out of the beak. The furry mountain grumbled as the rest of the creatures attached themselves to its legs, quickly climbing up to reach the fur. It was trashing around, while Cake was still on his back, kicking at anything trying to get in through the door. His foot passed through one of the birds, the feathers evaporating around it. It cost him precious momentum and the bird was on top of him, beak and teeth itching for his face. There was something rank, something rotten stuck between them. Something rotten inside the bird, that oozed out at close contact. Cake reached for his ankle knife and struck it on the side of the bird's skull. The skull shattered to million little pieces and the arms and the beak and the breath disappeared into a mist, only to be replaced by another of the creatures trying to make its way in.

He chucked the knife he was still holding at the bird and hit it in the middle of its bare skull, then pulled the door shut and locked it. He could hear the four remaining hands clawing at the door and the plastic and metal screaming as they peeled off like so much wrapping paper.

Cake rushed to start the car. It wailed almost worse than the birds, complaining about the sudden wake up and inelegant handling, but agreed to a quick take off as soon as the bird creatures started making their way in front of the windshield.

He backed up hoping he wouldn't hit a tree and blasted the front lights, revealing a forest full of the creatures, an army of grotesque bird soldiers, trying to overpower the furry mountain and Cake's little camper van.

They were on top of the van already. He could hear the chittering and the tearing of the covers as claws pulled apart the car too swiftly. He saw the entrance route to the camp site he'd driven through and made a quick turn on the wheel. Bones rattled over the roof of the car. He punched the gas and accelerated through the low lying branches just next to the exist, breaking away both side mirrors in the tree trunks. The birch and oaks scraped the van clean like a sloppy car wash as he curved to the actual driveway, driving at a ridiculous speed. He could hardly control the vehicle, bumping along every minor pothole in the gravel road at a dangerous speed until he got to the main road leading towards Wytheville.

He wouldn't take his foot off the gas until the morning.

20.

The sunrise had never been more sorry than after a night of frantic driving. Cake's brain was a ball of confused bees, trying to make sense of what had happened, only knowing for sure that there were things that spoke and were not like bears at all. That would've liked to have killed him. Maybe eaten him. Yes, it felt very likely that they would've wanted to eat him too. And he didn't understand why. He still had trouble understanding anything he'd really seen.

Large birds. Large, possibly dead birds. With no feet. A big, moving mountain. Rotten smells, hands, a blur of events as things went south fast. The bees in his brain had driven themselves to exhaustion. The buzzing was slowly winding down, as Cake sat in the driver's seat of the raggedy camper van.

His foot eased off the gas as the sun climbed up higher, illuminating the day, pushing the darkness of the night back into whatever crack it had oozed out of.

The van puttered to a halt in front of a gas station.

Cake had little idea where he was anymore, since he'd just taken off and driven as fast and as far as he could.

The station looked... normal. The current normal. Not the normal he wanted, but the normal he had; without people but with many sharp teeth in the night. The station didn't seem to have sharp teeth. It was empty and quiet and one of the pumps was occupied by a car with its door hanging open.

He parked at another pump and climbed out. His feet nearly buckled from under him. They had no weight. His entire body had no weight. Everything felt strange, like he was watching himself through a TV screen walking to the emergency generator, turning it on, switching the power source and heading back to the van. It was all a lucid dream. It was all a dream until he saw what the camper looked like on the outside. The sides were almost completely peeled off, exposing wires and insulation. The solar panels on the roof had deep cuts. Half of them had been ripped off, and one was hanging by single screw, like a sad little pizza box.

His feet gave out and Cake slumped to the ground.

It had all been real.

He sat there on the ground, unable to move his hands or feet, just staring at nothing for a good ten minutes. Wind tousled his hair. Birds flew past high above him, making a racket.

He breathed in with his eyes closed, hands flopped onto the ground, listless.

A gray cat jumped out of the other car parked at the pumps and lazily stretched in the sun. It sauntered around his van like it was making an inspection. Noticing Cake sitting on the ground, it flounced over. The cat sat in front of him expectantly. Then it rolled over and casually sniffed at his knee, making the first move since he was not delivering on the expected social graces.

Cake stared at the cat unable to move.

His hands were numb. His body was numb. He was pretty sure his mouth was hanging open. There just was nothing in him right now to reach out to this little creature wanting to connect.

The cat waited for a cursory minute, then rolled back up and ran off into the grass chasing after whatever it was that cats saw that was always invisible to humans.

Cake's eyes followed the tip of the cat's tail until it was completely out of sight. His breath came back to him in sobs. He wiped his nose on his sleeve and exhaled a broken sigh.

No, no time to sit around. No time with things like that out in the night. They might be here. They might come. They might come now or when the sun set. He had to find a good place to hide. Hide, hide for the night and figure out what to do.

The emergency generator chugged along in the background as Cake made refills. He had no skills in fixing cars, but he could unhook the broken pizza box from the roof and use Gorilla tape to patch up and attach as much as he could of what was left of the sides of the van. The camper looked like a gothic Christmas present by the afternoon, but that was far better than important car bits suddenly just falling out of it while on the road.

He stocked extra knives from a near by fishing gear store. He'd have liked the knives to have longer blades, but he had more room for the short ones, so he didn't complain out loud, just under his breath. He moved around the unnamed town in a determined haze; Checking his notebook for new items he'd added. Anything that would be good for hitting or throwing. Sharpness was a plus.

He was out on the road by 3 pm, after a restless afternoon nap, heading further away from the woodlands. Now that he'd located where he'd ended up on the map during his blind drive at night, he needed a bigger city. That's where he was heading. And he needed to figure out what was nagging him at the bag of his mind. He was forgetting something and it felt important.

As the sun sank beyond the horizon and he was still a good hour away from Lexington, the clouds started taking on weird shapes. Cake stared at them through his adrenaline and coffee fueled determination. The clouds looked spindly. Spindly and twisted and dead, drawing dark cracks over the sunset. Like a dead tree obstinately reaching up.

Dead, gnarled up branches... Cake snapped out of his trance.

He'd seen those bird things before.

He pushed a CD in the player and let the cabin fill with melodic rock. He knew where he'd need to go but it would take at least two days of driving even if he could stay away from those things and take the shortest route. *Rock and roll don't fail me now.*

He didn't sleep for two days.

21.

The Newport town library was a red brick building with thick, lead glass windows that pleasantly twisted light during the daylight hours. The shapes they projected made the floor look like puddles. Cake remembered loving the little air bubbles trapped inside the glass as a kid. It made the windows more magical than the windows in their 1960s apartment building with the very ordinary, modern factory windows. These were sparkly, theirs were not. The library was a fantastical, flickering, kingdom with ogres and rogues and tiny dragons. Of course he and the other kids had been shushed every single time they'd played dragons and then some more dragons in the halls of the building. It was hard to play a dragon without roaring, but you had to be quiet, very quiet, and not be a dragon, run, or burn things inside a library.

Now he had entirely other reasons to stay very quiet in there.

Cake was curled up in the corner of a conference room squeezing a short gutting knife in his hand. He closed his eyes and let his senses wander around in the dark, listening intently. The books and shelves echoed only quiet and the shadows stood still.

Click. Rip.

Things moved outside, just under the window. Low to the ground.

Cake took shallow breaths, then relaxed again. It was probably a rat or a badger. He'd seen those every evening, making their way along the tall grass sprouting alongside the library walls. They probably had nests somewhere near as he might catch one groggily lumbering away out into the open in the morning. Wild animals didn't care about him staring at them. They'd hiss or stare back unblinking. Now he'd watch them from behind the window or, if he was just returning from his nightly round, from the other side of the road and think they had much more in common than he'd realized. He wasn't much of a morning person either. He'd wonder if they'd like coffee too. He hadn't gotten around offering them any yet, but it was a thing he considered.

There were a lot of things he considered now. It felt like an important ritual in keeping sane to question if badgers liked coffee.

An image of freshly baked donuts flitted through his mind and made his stomach churn involuntarily. He cursed under his breath. Both the growl and his cursing were things he didn't need to be doing right now and he pressed his back tighter against the wall, holding his breath again.

The night outside the window remained quiet.

No chattering. For the moment.

On his way back to Newport, he'd only stopped a few times, trying to hide away in the biggest cities he could find. Somewhere in the center where the tall buildings could shelter a grown man and his van behind their walls. Somewhere with plenty of corners and garages to conceal the ripped up camper. The first night he'd been brazen and left his van on an open parking area near a Walmart, while he tried to entertain himself inside the store for a while. His head and hands were weary from driving. He wasn't sure his eyes were working properly anymore and he knew he'd need to get more caffeine before he could continue driving. It would've been all too easy to mistake a ditch for a bridge in his condition.

The bird things had been there. They'd surrounded his camper at nightfall. He could only watch in horror as they circled it and clawed at the tapes, first inquisitively, then with determination trying to reach in for the wires and insulations and whatever it was that made a van tick. However intelligent they might've been, they couldn't figure out how to open the camper door (Cake still diligently locked his car even though there was very little chance passing wildlife would take it for a joyride). They'd been satisfied with mindlessly pecking at the tapes and wondering at the windshield wipers. One had pulled the left one off. The duct tape that help the camper together had been peeled away by morning, to reveal a decidedly inedible core.

They'd chattered among themselves in that awful gnashing sound he could feel all the way in his spine and remained there until the morning light had dispelled their bodies into the air. Cake had watched from his hiding place as the birds turned to stare at the rising sun in unison and one by one dissolved into dust and flies as the light hit them.

He had no idea if these were the same ones he'd met in the woods, following him hundreds of miles, or if they simply talked among each other. Were these new ones? Where did they come from? How many were there? He wasn't any smarter after the second night. All he knew for sure was that he wasn't going to get caught up anywhere near them at night. They were fast and strong and he only had two arms against their four each. And there were at least a dozen of them.

Maybe ten times dozen.

Maybe a hundred.

So he tried gassing up during the day and taking his breaks when it was light, but never sleeping, because if he fell asleep, they were sure to catch up. They'd found him hundreds of miles away from the woods. If they were looking for him specifically, they'd find him again.

In Newport, he'd ditched the camper on the outskirts of the city. The birdies - like he was now thinking of them in his slightly delirious state because it made him chuckle and maybe this was the first sign that everything was not okay with him - would find it anyway. They always found the camper for whatever reason. Cake was starting to suspect that there was some sort of dissemination of information between them. They talked. Did they have headquarters? A big boss bird telling them to go out and find him? He was a wanted man, which wasn't nearly as romantic or exciting as movies had made it out to be. It was actually stressing him out quite a bit. But then again, most people probably weren't wanted by giant carnivorous bird-monsters.

He'd made his way to the center of the city, hiding among the buildings again, picking up supplies on his way to the library.

The library had seemed like the only sensible choice with its heavy wooden doors and an abundance of books that could turn out to be useful in his situation. He'd locked himself in a conference room for a day and slept for the first time in a lifetime.

The sleep wasn't nearly as restful as he'd hoped, but his guts weren't letting him quite relax. Locked doors or not, daylight or not, there were things tugging at the back of his mind, things that felt like old habits about sleeping in enemy territory, that wouldn't let him do more than gather as much strength as he could from not moving around for a while.

When the night fell, he'd collect his knives, squeeze them close to his chest, and wonder about that familiarity as he sat in the darkness listening to the sounds coming from outside. He'd done this before, somehow, but he couldn't remember when or why.

You could always spot the birdies from their chattering. It was faint, but it was the one thing that gave them away since they had no feet and left no trails behind them. It was impossible to the tell where they'd passed through vegetation as their bodies seemed completely insubstantial.

He'd find gnawed up and torn cats and sometimes larger animals around the city during the day, but no footprints. The carcasses were the only trace they'd leave of themselves.

But they were there in Newport too.

He'd see flocks of them gliding from the shadows and back into them, the moonlight making them visible. Cake had picked up thermal night vision goggles from a hunting store and taken to wearing them at night when he was outside. They would pick up on any small animals out at night, but none of the other animals were ten foot tall birds. He couldn't see their bodies, but the goggles would pick up on the oblong shaped heads and a thin, glittery net where their spine might've been.

Cake couldn't decide if they looked more terrifying through the goggles or with his bare eyes.

He resolved that both were bad and he'd rather not see either if he had the choice.

By the third day at the library, he'd gathered a good arsenal of useful things in the backroom and set up cans and book stacks around as traps. Anything tried floating by them and he would know. He could sleep a bit better during the day. Research at the library's paranormal section had passed his idle hours between naps, but he'd found the section mostly filled with books about UFOs and Hitler conspiracy theories. There was a footnote of a few paragraphs in one book about a hairy "Boojum" that would wander around the Appalachian mountains, spying on mostly women, but the mountainous thing that tried to grab him was much more of a living fell than an 8 foot peeping tom, so Cake dismissed the few similarities and moved on. There were demon dogs, and birdwomen, and mothmen, but all of those had legs. The birdies didn't. Then he'd gotten distracted by some herbology books, but none of it was really helpful for repelling evil demon birds, so he only scribbled down notes on things that might be useful for clotting blood in case...

...in case he wasn't fast enough.

The thought gave him chills as the number of talons per bird flashed through his mind, and what they'd done to his poor van. His hand had slipped tentatively to the hilt of a knife on his side.

Eventually he'd just blitzed through the impressive collection of military manuals and set up the traps. The more traps, the less of a chance he'd have to wander in the dark looking for things to stop a possibly fatal bleeding, he reasoned.

***

The faints clinks stopped under the window and Cake took a sharp breath.

At the far end of the library a can of rocks toppled over as the string connected to it came loose and sent pebbles tumbling down the hallway. Cake held his breath. His heart stopped for far longer than he was comfortable with.

No rats squeaked, no cats stepped softly hugging the walls, indignant of his crude human contraptions. The night was still.

From the end of the long corridor, he could hear faint gnashing of teeth.

22.

Cake crawled under a side table clutching a knife to his chest. His breathing was much too loud. The fact that the bird things were inside the building didn't mean they'd know where he was yet, but he had to keep his breathing quiet. Not breathe. Stop entirely.

He was desperately trying to cover his mouth with his free hand, curled up to a ball in the furthest corner of the room.

In the shadows he couldn't even see himself. The darkness was profound and complete.

The chattering remained at the end of the hall. He heard metal scraping against bone, as the empty can was being moved around. The few stones still inside it tumbled over banging against each other louder than anything he'd heard in his life. How could a few small rocks make such an ear-bursting noise, he thought biting down on his lips, as fear creeped around the building, scraping at the books, gnashing its teeth together making that obscene wet sound. It was a primal noise he felt rather than heard. Like they were always chewing on something.

His mother always said chewing with his mouth open was a nasty habit. No one wanted to see what was inside his mouth. He'd deliberately noshed his food twice as loud, with his mouth twice as wide, and went to bed without dessert that night.

Maybe giant murder birds didn't have caring mothers. They probably didn't have dessert either. Or he was the dessert.

Cake squeezed his eyes shut.

The chittering moved away from the hallway, becoming just a faint echo. He could hear the empty can dropping to the floor and rolling against a wall.

It was a good while before he dared to breathe again.

After what felt like about twenty minutes but could just as easily have been ten or 120, Cake unfurled himself from under the table. The chatter had moved past his window, but hadn't stopped and hadn't come back. They could still be around, he thought, as he couldn't rely on his mediocre hearing alone. He also couldn't check anything from under the table, so he carefully crawled from his hiding place and, flat against the walls, and made his way to the roof of the library with the night vision goggles.

The winds were getting harsh as fall was moving in, but he barely noticed how it whipped his bare arms red as he observed the streets below from the roof.

There were several murder birds floating around in front of the building. They were moving away in a group, taking the smaller streets north from the library. Cake moved to the west side and noticed two smaller groups there, floating to the same direction.

They weren't heading to the woods. The woods were over to the other side of the city.

"Where are you creepers going...?" Cake muttered to himself, then quickly ducked down realizing his mistake. *Shit. No talking. NO TALKING!*

The groups had stopped and were eyeing at the building as he carefully peeked at them behind a ventilation shaft. They soon resumed in the direction they had been heading before, and Cake sank back down pulling the goggles off with trembling hands. He couldn't stop shaking.

There must've been two dozen of the creatures in all those groups together. He couldn't defend himself properly against three. Taking on ten or more would be the end of him.

He felt sick.

But where were they going?

He saw more groups moving in the same direction the original three had gone, on the east side of the building. They weren't picking up animals like they normally would and they weren't leaving the group, patrolling individually, like they had done on other nights. More and more birds were uniformly flowing in the same direction. Cake could see nothing particular in the horizon, mostly because it was dark, but also because there were taller buildings between the library and wherever they were going. He could just see faintly glowing lines where the streets were as the creatures moved from individual groups into longer strings of single files.

At the south side he could see a tail end to their stream.

Cake climbed down from the roof.

Trying to trail hulking murder birds at night when you didn't have actual night vision, or 4 arms and a lust for fresh kills, was almost harder than trying not breathe.

Cake stumbled over rubble and vines and tufts of grass wildly poking through the sidewalks, trying to keep eye contact with the last of the groups. He felt like a blind elephant in a china shop. Everything he did was too loud, even blinking. He kept constantly dodging behind buildings and trashcans, and was sweating so much he was sure if his footsteps didn't give him away, the smell of his sweat would. It was overpowering even for him. But he kept reminding himself that most things felt much stronger to the person with anxiety, than they were to anyone without, and he was definitely experiencing a moment of anxiety right now.

They moved out of the main streets and glided into the suburbs, and his perspiring became worse as things to hide behind became more sparse. The creatures drifted along the streets chattering among themselves while he tried hiding behind flimsy fences and bushes, pretending to be a lawn ornament once when he was sure a murder bird was staring directly at him. It stopped and turned to face Cake, hovering quietly over the feral lawn. It was definitely looking directly at him, and it was taking everything Cake had to try and stop his skeleton from escaping out of his mouth in terror. Who knew what was going on in those bald skulls of theirs. He couldn't read their eyes since they didn't have any. Or facial expressions, since they didn't have faces either.

The bird stared directly at him for a moment, then turned away and floated after its group.

Maybe their night vision was as poor as his was.

Maybe theirs was worse since they had no eyes.

Maybe he wasn't the dessert after all.

The lines floated down familiar streets. As the last bird disappeared around the corner of a house, Cake realized where he was. This was were he had been heading himself. The birds got here first.

The unusually wide empty space between the neighboring houses and the 'Turnop For President' sign that was still there, four years after the election supposedly took place. He looked at the yard sign, clearly left out for nothing but to spite everyone who disagreed with the sentiment.

Cake squited at Miss Bannister's house at the end of the cul-de-sac. A faintest glow emanated from her backyard.

The grass on the neighbors' yards was slowly starting to tinge more yellow, but it was still long and healthy, swallowing mail boxes and low fences under its lusciousness. The shrubberies had taken over foot paths and trees were arching dangerously over the roofs and windows, intimidating the man-made houses into submission in front of nature.

But the grass around Miss Bannister's house was dead. It was more than dead; there was no grass there to be dead. There was nothing but gray dust surrounding her porch and her foot path. The bushes covering the sides of the house, the ones that used to provide the football field she called her backyard some privacy, were black stalks with not a leaf or a blossom. They'd died where they stood. And between her dead grass and the neighbor's rather normal, if outgrown, lawns, there was a clear line, like someone had taken a ruler and decided the grass on one side was to be torched.

Cake leaned against the wall of the Bannister house and took a deep breath.

He peeked around the corner.

The field was gray and empty with nothing alive for as far as the eye could see, right up until the interstate that framed her lot.

In the middle of it, the bird creatures were hovering in a circle around something. Something bright.

Cake squinted and felt like he could see what was glowing, but the wall of wispy ghost-bodies was obscuring whatever it was they were circling. The chattering had congealed into a singular hum that was by far worse than the wet gnashing of a lone demon beak. They were moving around in a circle, with creatures occasionally breaking away from it and trying to move further in, but being pushed back and being unable to move past a certain point.

Whatever was there, Cake needed to know. It seemed to repel the birds and they were certainly much too attracted to it for it to be just another cat or a squirrel. Whatever it was, he needed it. But there were dozens upon dozens of them there and he was all alone and whatever feeble weapons he'd have against them, he'd left at the library.

Cake patted down his sides trying to find anything he could use; a long knife, a camera, a can of soup. He had nothing but a knife.

He'd left everything at his library hideout.

There was nothing to use as a weapon and nothing to use a distraction and frankly, after all his careful planning at the library, this seemed like an impossibly stupid situation he'd put himself in. He didn't even have a plan for a situation like this. Bum-rush all hundreds of them? In this economy? He could wait until morning. As far as plans went, picking the only one that didn't involve certain death seemed reasonable.

Cake pulled back behind the corner, then took off back to the center, trying to silently move between the houses, eyes still peeled at any birdies that might be making rounds in the dark.

23.

By noon, Cake was back at the Bannister house. He'd roped knives around his ankles and on his hips in makeshift bandoliers he feared were less practical than they looked.

They looked very impractical.

He was holding a composite baseball bat in one hand slung easily on his shoulder. The weight of it felt comforting even as he regretted not taking the time to practice with any kind of a gun. But a bat could smash things on a larger area and maybe keep anything carnivorous at an arms length. And it wouldn't run out of bullets.

The cul-de-sac looked only marginally more appealing in daylight than it had in the middle of the night. The houses were weathered, windows dimmed by dust, undergrowth utterly out of control. No cats or mice or rats stirred the grass outside the dead zone, and definitely not inside it. If a place could feel like a corpse without there being any corpses in it, that's how this place felt, Cake thought. He briefly wondered what it would be like to feel a corpse and managed to panic himself out momentarily.

The grass around the Bannister house was still nothing but ash. Cake poked at it with the tip of the bat, turning over a stone jutting out of the dusty earth, and found nothing but more gray under it.

The ground was well and truly dead. Like it had been purposefully leeched of all life. Not even bugs crawled from under the upturned rock, and there were always things living under rocks.

Cake stroked his beard crouched down next to the rock, looking at the unnatural dearth of life.

He felt he was unqualified to make assessments on most things he'd seen in the past week. Or in the past year, but this seemed like a more bad and not-naturally occurring situation right here, than he'd ever seen.

The black limbs of the bushes broke away into dust as he pushed past them into the back yard. He could see a vaguely circular area roughly in the middle of the field and something in the middle of it.

Both hands on the bat, he approached it cautiously.

The gray dust on the ground gave away to a perfectly smooth circle. The diameter was approximately the size of a luxury hot tub. It had seemed a much larger area last night, which made him think there were much more of the creatures than he'd first estimated. Neither of these thoughts pleased him much.

The edges of the circle were smudged with something crispy and brown. Almost black. And inside the circle were markings drawn in the same color. There were 5 smooth stones set at even distances from each other around the circle, just inside the dark brown circle.

Cake remembered how the creatures had tried approaching the center but been pushed back like there was something preventing them from entering.

He kneeled to the ground and waved his hand over the lines, but nothing happened. He tried passing his hand over the stones and again, nothing happened. It didn't seem to react to him in any way, or there was just nothing there anymore and whatever it was the birdies had been trying to get at, they'd succeeded in getting and had flown away with it last night.

Cake got up and glared at the circle.

This could be bad or it could be good, or it could be very bad in a way he couldn't understand.

He paced around the ring.

There was a shiny tomato-soup can at the center of it, standing perfectly calm and ordinary among all the weirdness of the entire set up.

Cake strode to the middle, careful not to step on any of the markings, and poked the can with his bat. It clang hollow but didn't move. He crouched down and tried moving it by hand, but the can seemed nailed to the very base rock itself.

"Could be an art installation," he thought out loud, then quickly glanced around.

Small birds were sitting quietly in a far off bush, tilting their heads. The bright of the day was indifferent, nor did it seem to have an issue with this installation. Whatever it was. Right now it just existed in perfect harmony with this dead and unnatural spot.

She could've burnt her backyard to install this.

Cake rubbed his forehead.

She could've burnt her backyard with napalm just to install a weird, semi-pagan light art installation with its own power source and the murder birds were attracted to the lights. And you could be trying to rationalize things because it's been getting weird and scary and you don't want it to be those things, buddy.

"It's probably not an art installation," Cake muttered, marching back out of the circle, "how do I make it go?" He flopped down on the ground scratching his head.

The stone he was sitting in front of was white and smooth, with little sparkly flecks in it, catching the daylight in a rainbow. He rubbed the stone's surface absentmindedly, and let his eyes wander over the markings on the ground. They didn't seem even vaguely familiar. Not in the same way the bird creatures had when they talked. That had triggered something. He was almost sure they hadn't spoken English, but somehow he'd understood the few words they'd said. Understood and heard them on a bone level that made him want to pull his ears off. Their language was almost obscene to listen to.

No, this was not like that. This was just... alien.

"Maybe everyone's been abducted by aliens," he muttered under his breath. "Big, hairy, moss aliens took over the mountains. Murder birds everywhere else. Yup... aliens."

Cake sighed. He let his bat drop to the ground.

A little wind rustled the birds off the distant bush and twirled the dust in the ring. His eyes caught something flapping at the other side of the circle.

Something he hadn't noticed before.

Cake got up and strode next to it.

It was a piece of paper stuffed under a red rock. It was badly weather-worn, the text bleached to pale green under the seasons and the paper ragged from rain. It looked like a page from a magazine. He could vaguely make out the shapes of greenish dogs as the ink had been bleached by at least one fall and a winter.

Cake turned the paper around in his hand. The backside of it, the one that'd been buried against the ground, was still almost fresh. Over the print that had fragments of dog food ingredients, were words smudged in dark brown blocks. He turned the paper around to make the letters stand the right side up.

"Ti-... tiõrv? Pue-...Tiõrv pue'ttem!"

The can shot up into the sky as something small but powerful went off under it filling the field in blinding light. A shock wave punched the air out of his chest and Cake could feel his body becoming weightless, the center of the circle moving further and further away before he realized the circle wasn't moving and he wasn't standing but the horizon was fast moving up and his body moving down like so much listless matter, plummeting from the easy weightlessness back down as gravity finally grabbed a hold of him, before the ground knocked him unconscious.

24.

His face was wet and hurting as Cake finally came to. Every part of his body felt bruised, glued to the gray dust by hurt. And his face was getting wetter. Was it raining? He tried swallowing and even that hurt.

He heard breathing next to his ear, then something wet touched his earlobe. It jolted him back to his senses and his eyes shot open, the rum old instinct of sleeping in enemy territory kicking in. The sky was dusky and between his face and the sky there was a pair of dark brown puppy eyes.

The dog licked his face again. It smelled like kibbles and ham if both had been stored up someone's butt.

It whined and paced nervously pack and fort, pawing at his arm.

Cake forced himself up even if that hurt him more than lying down, feeling every bruise from being at the epicenter of an explosion. He squinted but couldn't see the can anywhere. Whatever it was, it was gone. They were alone in a dead, empty field. The dog whined nervously.

"Ok, ok, I'm up. Good boy," he reached out to pat the dog but it ducked his hand.

It was really more of a puppy. A tiny beagle-like puppy in light beige. Where a beagle would've had dark patches, this puppy was just two different shades of light beige with large amber puppy eyes, and a slightly scruffy looking face.

He hadn't seen a puppy or a dog in ages, now that he thought about it. The last time was somewhere in South America. While he was traveling through the US and Canada though...

Cake quickly pushed the images out of his mind. The dogs had mostly been indoors or chained up when the people disappeared. That was all there was to it.

He reached out gently with his palm up and tried a friendly tone.

"Here, bud," his voice came out in a croak. It scared both him and the puppy. It'd been a while since he'd talked to another living thing and not just muttered into his beard, so his voice was hoarse from disuse. "It's ok, buddy," he tried again, and this time his voice didn't break and the puppy remained still, letting him reach its chin. Cake stroked the dog's chin lightly and its eyes relaxed bit by bit. It dropped its head and sniffed around his fingers before letting him move his hand to scratch it behind its ear.

"You're a good pupper, aren't you? Yes, you're a good little boy," Cake cooed gently.

Everything in his legs felt smushed up and his back was a raw steak, but in his heart a little flicker of tenderness swell as the dog approached him, sat next to him, and was now fully reveling in the petting.

"Where did you come from, little friend? You look very young, where's mama and papa dog?" Cake tried coaching the dog, noticing it didn't have a collar around its neck. It could've been born wild from some lucky dogs that got away.

The dog blinked.

Cake realized it wasn't going to answer him in so many words and started looking around the field to spot if there were more wild dogs around. He saw no dogs, just a sun rapidly disappearing behind the horizon and dark clouds rolling over the sky.

Weird, spindly clouds reaching from the edges of the night to cover the stars. His heart started beating faster.

"Come on, we need to get out of here, pup. It's not safe here."

He looked around desperation tickling at the edges of his calmness. The only house close enough was the Bannister one. Aside from the rickety tool shed, he had few options.

He pushed himself off the ground, every bone in his body telling him how walking was a bad idea. "Come. Gotta go. Now," he motioned the dog.

The puppy followed him wagging its tail.

The back door was closed and so was the front. The dark was rolling in faster than Cake could anticipate, and the shadows were growing longer around the houses. Branches were reaching out towards the last remaining strips of light like greedy hands asking for salvation. Soon the neighborhood was bathing in a strange red light.

Cake felt anxiety grip his guts harder than the bruises had. They had to get in somewhere. Now.

He'd tried hard avoiding damaging anyone's property at any time, when sleeping on strange couches in strangers' empty homes or 'borrowing' food from abandoned stores and cupboards, but desperate times called for more violence; He pulled up one of Miss Bannister's metallic deck chairs and flung it against the screen door. The plastic webbing came loose and flopped to the side like a newspaper page in the wind. He picked up the chair again, flung it, this time managing to break the backdoor lock enough that when he gave it a good kick, the door gave in with a snap. He picked the puppy under his arm and dashed inside the dark house.

As much as they were both in quite a bit of danger right now, Cake couldn't help but feel a little thrilled being inside the house. He'd often wondered about the place. Miss Barrister was a weird old lady and she was sure to have weird old lady hobbies, and Cake had sometimes distracted himself thinking about what kind of a person would bury a gigantic bird skull in their equally enormous backyard. Or have pet goats in their suburban bungalow. Would she have more than just two kids? Maybe lizards or a cactus in pajamas? Would she have a collection of rudely shaped sea shells or golf clubs she'd stolen?

He'd wondered, because it was a distraction, and he'd wondered about all the lives of the disappeared people whose houses he'd visited. He'd made up their lives to be elaborate and filled with soap opera details, because aside from the frequent yelling and incest in soap operas, average lives had complex connections. But he hadn't <u>really</u> expected there to ever be anything more than something slightly quirky about Miss Bannister.

He didn't expect her walls to be covered in bones.

They weren't just particularly interesting bones or like trophy skulls. No, it was more like the pictures of catacombs he'd seen where entire walls were piles of skulls, and chandeliers were made from skulls, and all ledges and seats were just more skulls. Mostly she didn't seem to have skulls. Just a lot of straight bones from... lord knows where. From humans? Animals? Something else. They covered the walls in layers like wallpaper. The floor has covered in bright red leather carpet and there were Ikea furniture sprinkled here and there in a jarring contrast to the dusty-yellow bones covering the walls.

Cake recognized a sofa as the one he'd also had in his old apartment. Only his had been green. This one had a white, betasseled upholstery with tiny, preppy flowers dotting it.

"What on earth... Miss Barrister, you were up to some shit," Cake breathed rubbing a lamp shade between his fingers. It felt waxy and looked like it had a weird webbing-print on it, only the webbing was embossed on both sides.

The puppy wagged its tail against his chest.

"Wait, waitwaitwait, buddy," Cake told the dog. "I'm still sore."

The puppy pulled its ears back looking guilty.

"And we need to be quiet." He raised his finger to his lips. "There's bad stuff outside, understand?" *There might be bad stuff on the inside too*.

The puppy broke out in a puppy smile. Cake couldn't help grinning back at it. They were going to get along just fine, his new friend and him. Assuming they weren't both dead. That would make them not fine at all.

He moved charily through the house, finding only more bones and mismatched minimalist Swedish furniture. The kitchen was a den of ants. The cupboards had several opened boxes of cookies that would probably only be good for the ants that'd already claimed them. A few larger jars that smelled like moonshine, were sitting on the counter. The bedroom was light blue and possibly the only room on the floor with no bones covering the walls. Just a suspiciously life-like stuffed rabbit in the middle of a neatly made bed.

The house didn't even smell particularly weird. A familiar heavy, lingering smell that gave him a headache after a while. Opium. The perfume, not the eau de toilette or the drug. Cake's first employer had worn the scent and the smell immediately connected with his first job interview where he'd struggled with a splitting headache. But of course you never said to your boss they smelled bad. You just leaned back a lot.

In this house, Cake wondered if it was really the perfume Miss Bannister used. The décor didn't strike him as the kind that would belong to an Opium-user. The perfume or otherwise.

The last door lead to the basement.

Cake stood before it, puppy under one arm, a large, red candle he'd found in the kitchen in the other.

He hesitated for a moment before grabbing the handle. People always hid the worst things either in the attic or the basement. Of course it was almost a rhetorical question if he actually wanted to know what she'd hidden in the basement. There were few things that could've persuaded him from peeking in, like possibly a bio hazard symbol or a door made from corpses, screaming when you touched them.

He looked at the bone-covered walls, but could see neither of those things in so many words, so down they went into the dark of the basement, as the wind picked up outside and carried with it distant sounds.

The basement was littered with computer parts. There was a three screen set up and a central unit the size of a small closet standing in the corner. Papers and books covered the floor and table surfaces, with empty tea cups balancing on top of empty tea cups. The cups were all very delicate, with different kinds of hand painted flowers, and gilded rims.

Cake leaned down and a faint smell of mint greeted him. The waste basked under the computer desk was filled with used tea bags.

He felt a twinge of envy looking at the computer set up in the dim light of the candle. It was truly impressive. And now a chunk of useless garbage. No electricity, no use for computers. The thousands of dollars Miss Bannister must've sunk into this unit, whether she was a hacker or a gaming enthusiast - a thought that pulled the corner of Cake's mouth into a secret smirk - didn't matter anymore. The hardware was just junk. A pretty paperweight. Or a paper holder for her books and prints and tea cups.

He turned from the dead screens to follow the trail of papers and clippings flowing from the table on to the wall, red marker scribbled all over them, highlighting passages, circling others. The furthest wall of the basement was plastered entirely with news items and pages from... something. They were copies of books, maybe? The news clippings showed people in white robes. Gaunt and ostensibly cheery people, carrying signs about veganism and yoga.

Oh god.

Cake leaned closer.

Oh god, I know her. I know them!

The Children Of the Blessed Calm. Every news item was about the Children Of the Blessed Calm. The ones where the cult wasn't mentioned, Cake assumed the people had some connection to them regardless, as the same people kept appearing in all of the photographs. The same names were underlined. News about new chapters being founded, protest being held. The cult being granted an official church status, and a longer full color article from TIME-magazine detailing the construction of their new mega-sanctuary.

Between the news articles were photocopies of book pages. They were dim, and symbols and words had been traced over with green highlighter to make them more legible.

The same words as on the slip he'd found outside made an appearance, but so did many others. Symbols that meant nothing to him and didn't look like any he'd seen on Wiccan books or websites.

Cake considered how many Wiccan books or websites he'd seen.

The answer was one of each.

He felt mildly displeased with himself. He had no frame of reference. But his library would have books and he could compare these if he just took some with him...

The puppy let out concerned bark.

"What is it? You see a rat?" Cake looked down at the pup.

The dog started wiggling under his arm trying to break free.

"Hey, hold on, you can't go-"

The puppy growled at the stairs.

"Oh no...," he whispered grabbing the pup by the nose. "Oh no. You need to be quiet." He looked the dog in the eyes and saw a glimmer of understanding there. Enough to make him loosen his grip.

"You can't make a sound," he whispered.

Cake stared up into the ceiling listening to the wind howling outside. Things were moving just outside the house. Outside the broken back door.

He blew out the candle and cautiously rose up the stairs, pressing his body against the wall and stopping at every step to listen.

To listen to the chatter outside.

At the top of the stairs they stopped. He could just pull the cellar door closed. He could just do that and hope the birdies didn't come in. Hope they weren't smart enough to put two and two together about the baseball bat that was now laying somewhere near their precious circle, and the broken back door creaking and banging against its frame in the wind.

But then they'd be stuck in the cellar if the creatures did come in. They'd have nowhere to back into, and he had no space to throw things. There would be one point of exist and that's where the birds would come in.

He shifted uneasily on his feet.

They'd have to try sneaking out.

Cake set the puppy down and once again, put a finger on his lips telling it to keep quiet. It sat down and tilted its head expectantly. Cake nodded to reaffirm how good the dog was being. Then he slipped out the cracked cellar door. The puppy followed, stepping carefully with its oversized baby paws. Not a floor board creaked. The only thing filling his ears was the violent rushing of blood through his veins.

They both stood in the hallway staring at the front door.

He could see moonlight casting shadows through the windows. The shadows had beaks and many talons, and moved silently across the frames. Cake and the dog stayed still, listening, as the chattering moved past the shafts of light, and along the side of the house. More shadows kept streaming by. He wished he could've seen how they were reacting to the missing can in the back yard, but more importantly, he wished this wasn't the place they were hiding right now.

The gnashing glided along the walls of the building, like sticky syrup with teeth in it, and Cake had a hard time controlling his revulsion. He glanced down on the puppy and saw it bearing its little puppy teeth, the little snout twitching to bark.

Cake shook his head trying to look angry through his terror. *No*, he mouthed. The dog pulled back, looking up at him, a furry beige bellhop waiting for a command. Cake wagged his finger in a way he hoped the dog would understand. It seemed like such a smart little pup, but some things just didn't easily translate.

The shadows outside the window stopped.

The gnashing and clicking didn't. The skeletal shadows cocked their heads and twitched their claws in unnatural silhouettes as Cake and the puppy stood frozen.

Sweat poured from every pore on his skin, down Cake's back, and glued his shirt on his body. *Please don't hear us please don't hear us can you smell us please don't please do-*

A moment of absolute silence followed as the shadows tilted their heads back and forth. Then their line started moving again.

As soon as the last shadow passed around the corner, Cake motioned for the dog.

He unlocked the front door and peeked outside.

The street was dark and empty. Nothing was moving, not the leaves, not the grass, not the shadows under rooftops.

Cake swallowed.

He cautiously took a step forward, when the wind picked up, blew right past him into the house and through the broken back door. The door clanged against the frame with a loud bang shattering his heart. *Shit! Shitshitshit!* They had to go. Now. Run!

He grabbed the puppy and made a dash for the nearest house but halfway through the wide open space that was the end of the street, the shadows started materializing, branches molding into arms and heads, leaves stretching into beaks.

The eyes remained hollow. Empty sockets peering at them through the night as the gigantic birds slowly surrounded Cake and the dog.

He set the dog down, giving it a sad smile.

"We might not both make this, little buddy," he whispered. "Run while you can."

The pup looked at him wagging its tail.

Cake let his hands fall down, looking for the nearest hilt, eyeing at the five birds in front of him. He could hear the chattering behind him and the words forming at the back of his head.

"Flesh...," the words echoed in his bones. "Eat...," and eating had never sounded more revolting in his ears.

Why they simply circled him, he didn't know. They were slowly surrounding him but maintaining a distance, while his fingers frantically gripped for knives from the bandoliers.

"Well? What are you waiting for?!"

Did they need to toy with their prey before eating it? Cake had pulled out two sturdy knives and, with his back hunched, was bracing his body for impact.

There was a shattered hacking sound. Like a cat coughing up a fur ball, if the fur was glitter.

The line of birds waved back as the hacking sound became stronger. Cake swung his head around trying to locate the source, his eyes catching a coughing puppy. It was retching up something green and translucent, looking like it was choking. The tiny body was gasping for air, pulling it in in gulps as the small rib cage swell. It swell beyond anything normal. The skin was ballooning between the ribs as the dog gasped for more and more air and a green glow shone through the skin between the ribs. The dog was glowing from the inside.

Finally it barked. A deep, bellowing roar belonging to an animal ten times the size rushed out from the tiny body pushing forward a giant green orb. The orb hit the nearest bird creature and incinerated it in a blast of green flames.

Now the rest of them stopped hesitating as talons came lunging at them from all sides.

He ducked to the side, grabbing the puppy as he rolled and flung his two knives blindly. Both hit a bird, but only one shattered a skull. The other flew through the creature's opaque body crashing through a window behind it.

Cake tried jumping over the birds as they went low but got caught by flailing talons and dragged back to the ground where the puppy was already hacking up another green bolt. Another bird went up in flames and the chattering was reaching a fever pitch as more creatures poured from the sides of the houses. With a swift kick, Cake shattered two more skulls while his knives found their aims and more creatures disintegrated back into the shadows, but there were still too many. Too many talons pulling at him, giant claws tearing into his skin like fish hooks, the sheer number of them was overwhelming him no matter how accurate his aim, and he was lying on the ground now, trying to avoid the teeth the claws, protecting his head while kicking anything he could. He couldn't see the dog anywhere and a terrible resignation spread into his body.

A bright light spread across the attacking horde.

It wasn't green, it was pure white. It dispersed the bodies and turned the beaks and the arms and the little knives slicing through his flesh into dust.

Cake was lying on the ground as ashes gently fell from the night sky. His hair was covered in ashes. His face was bloodied and striped black from the falling soot. He could only see the night and the stars above him, and only hear the silence outside of him as his heart thundered inside his chest.

Rushing foot steps echoed on the asphalt towards Cake. Something was coming, but he couldn't move. His skin felt like a million open wounds and the ground was the only place that didn't hurt and he couldn't move now and maybe he could never move again, and the foot steps were very close.

A face appeared between the sky and him.

He couldn't see the features clearly in the night. He could only hear a voice.

"Are you ok?" came from a distance.

He was hallucinating.

"Hey, are you alright?" A snapping of fingers in front of his face. "Blink once for yes. Twice for no. Are you alive?"

A woman's face came into focus. It was round and pleasant, with a short, button nose and a halo of kinky hair. Her skin was so dark, he had a hard time making out details in the night.

Cake blinked once.

"Good! Goddamn that would've sucked if you were dead," the voice was from a little further off now. "Come on, get up. We can't stay here," his hands grabbed hers and he was on his feet looking down on the first living human he'd seen in over a year and she was short and determined and she'd saved his life somehow. He lunged forwards wrapping his arms around her, a real live human. He was grinning. His face hurt from everything but he was sure he was grinning, squeezing her tight and bloody and now he couldn't tell anymore because tears were rolling down his cheeks, obscuring everything but her warmth and he was hugging her and crying in ugly sobs as her hands held him tight. This was real. She was there.

Someone had found him.

"What are you doing here? No one is supposed to be here anymore."

The adventure will continue in
Layer Cake

www.ingramcontent.com/pod-product-compliance
Lightning Source LLC
Chambersburg PA
CBHW061435150726
47987CB00001B/218